MW00323986

Justifiable

Murder in the Mountain State
A Novel

By Bob Irelan
Author of *Angel's Truth*

Outer Banks Publishing Group
Raleigh/Outer Banks

What others are saying about *Justifiable*
Five-Star Reviews on Amazon ★★★★★

Justifiable -- A really fine read

Justifiable is a remarkably good book. The police-procedural structure is masterful. It puts you in the action and makes you feel almost a part of the team. The "story" part is even better. The characters are deftly drawn, especially Ella Mae, and the bits of humor dropped in help to move the story along delightfully. It is a really fine read. - Ron Rhody

A book you can't put down

What a joy to read. Literally couldn't put it down. Multiple tension points keep your attention all the way to the final page. Outstanding character development of key players. This is the author's second book. I'm ready for # 3. - Beulah S. Coyne

Fast-moving and believable

Bob Irelan has done it again with his second mystery. Justifiable is a delightful book, a pleasure to read. The plot and action move quickly but not so fast that the reader does not get to know the main characters, solid citizens in a small town who support each other. - A.J.

He got what he deserved

There has been a murder in town . . . and not a soul mourns. How does a (mystery) writer keep you interested when no one wants the crime solved? He takes you inside the investigation . . . he introduces you to the people of the town . . . he lets you see why the victim was so universally reviled, and . . . finally, he surprises you at the end and makes you wonder why you didn't see that coming. - Bobbie Fite

Justifiable -- a great read

What a wonderful mystery! I was sure I knew who did it but, was I wrong, Can't wait for Bob's next book. - Joanne G.

Good read

Bob's gift is keeping us glued. Even though most of the story is about "good guys win in the end," I couldn't put it down! - Jess Erickson

A feel good crime

Enjoyable, easy read. Very identifiable and relatable characters in a realistic plot for the U.S. today. In the end, the reader felt good. - Amazon Kindle customer

Wonderful read!

A great read. A murder mystery but a very pleasant experience. Did not put it down. Easy to read, interesting situation, and things do turn out quite wonderfully. . . . West Virginia is quite different in many ways and this book does a wonderful job of communicating some of the very generous and human qualities in the culture. The book leaves an enjoyable glow. - David Geary

FIRST EDITION – September 2020

Library of Congress Control Number: 2020943766

ISBN 13 - 978-1-7341687-6-1
eISBN – 978-1-0059058-4-2

For Barbara

ACKNOWLEDGMENTS

This story and its characters are made up, creations of my imagination. But the several people who guided and encouraged me along the way are real. They are:

Judith Embree, a dear friend for more than ten years, who contributed good ideas, fresh approaches, and careful reading.

Melissa Irelan, my wonderful daughter-in-law, who lent her keen eye, good judgment, and questioning mind.

And Publisher Anthony Policastro, who — once again — did the heavy lifting of converting a raw manuscript into a book.

I am indebted to each of them.

Principal Characters
(In order of appearance)

Don Blackford, Superintendent, West Virginia State Police
Spence Atkins, Homicide Chief, WVSP
Russell Kincaid, 3rd generation owner, Kincaid Fabricators
Frank Wharton, Police Chief, Waterford, WV
Beverly Kincaid, Russell's ex-wife
Jeffrey "Junior" Kincaid, Russell's father
Florence Treadwell, Junior Kincaid's executive assistant
Jake Walter, Kincaid plant manager
Steve Insley, Mayor of Waterford
Darlene Davis, owner of Darlene's Dream Diner
Dagwood, Darlene's African Grey parrot
Ella Mae Gurney, Wally Hitchcock & Phil Sweeney, Kincaid
   employees
Elise Fortney, Russell's secretary
Al Donaldson, President, Allied Manufacturing
Roscoe Barnes, Detective, Cleveland Police Department
Michael Obitz, Prominent lawyer/former Attorney General
Sherman Wilson, Russell's lawyer

CHAPTER 1

February 2017

"The way I see it, we've got something like 200 suspects."

Don Blackford shook his head, interlocked his fingers as he always did when he was trying to figure something out, and stared across the desk at the person he'd known, worked alongside, and trusted for 20 years.

"Yeah, and that's on the low side. You're counting only the most recent employees," Spence Atkins replied, heaving a sigh as he pulled his chair closer to Blackford, the Superintendent of the West Virginia State Police. "It doesn't count family, former friends, retirees, lovers, and anybody else who was stiffed by the bastard."

The "bastard" was Russell Kincaid. His naked body had floated ashore near the Wilkens Ferry Landing the previous day. Even though the corpse was bloated from being in the water, the face had been recognized immediately by the Waterford police chief, Frank Wharton, and the identity confirmed by Kincaid's ex-wife, Beverly. The report from Chief Wharton was that Beverly struggled unsuccessfully to shed a tear when viewing photos of the body. One thing was certain: the hatred toward Kincaid was broad, deep, and in Beverly's case, still very personal.

"We've got a job to do," Blackford said, "and the hell of it is that no one wants us to do it. They figure he got what he deserved. An eye for an eye ... justice done ... closure."

"That's for sure," Atkins, now the department's homicide chief, replied. "I'll be friggin' shocked if any witness steps forward."

Blackford nodded. "Remember that movie, 'Spartacus'? The part where Kirk Douglas, God rest his soul, faces certain death, and one after another gladiator comes to his defense by saying, 'I am Spartacus'? Remember that? When and if we zero in on whoever did this, I can see that happening."

Spence Atkins nodded but didn't say anything, smoothing his mustache and visualizing that famous scene.

"But, old pal," Blackford said as he picked up his indelibly-stained "WVU" (West Virginia University) coffee mug and took a swig, "a murder's been committed. The son of a bitch has a hole in his head, then was tossed in the river. We've gotta go after this one like we do any other. That's why they pay us the big bucks." The last sentence produced a chuckle from Atkins.

CHAPTER 2

Waterford is a town of about 2,800 people and, like so many small West Virginia communities, is situated alongside a river. In Waterford's case, it's the Maplethorn, which flows west into the Ohio. Wedged between a couple of unnamed mountain ridges, the town is bisected by a rail line on which a single freight train runs once each morning and evening. A two-lane, two-stop-light road leads six miles to the Interstate. Locals describe Waterford as "removed, not remote."

Small farms, two- or three-acre single-family lots, and manufactured home neighborhoods dot the countryside beyond the town limits. Like so many other communities in the Bible Belt, Waterford has a surfeit of churches — 19 at last count — representing most known denominations as well as some invented locally. It takes nothing more than a minor disagreement with a pastor for several families to break away and form their own church.

Kincaid Fabricators came to town in the 1960s. Until then, Waterford had only the essentials in terms of commercial activity — a post office, bank, drug store, hardware store, grocery store, beauty parlor, gas station, diner, and bar.

At first, many locals weren't sure they wanted a factory like the one Jeffrey Kincaid, Russell's grandfather, promised to build. But it didn't take long for minds to change. Employment opportunities had been limited and young people couldn't wait to leave for the promise of a better future somewhere else. Kincaid brought stability and a sense of pride and belonging by providing good-paying jobs, promoting from within, and generously giving back to the community. Over the years, the company expanded a public park, built a library, and even added additional classrooms at the elementary and middle schools. It was not uncommon for entire families to work at Kincaid — father and son in casting or finishing, for example, and mother and daughter in accounting or shipping.

Old man Jeffrey Kincaid founded the business to produce a high-pressure valve he'd invented that doubled the force and, therefore, the range of fire hoses. Over time, the patented Kincaid valve became the standard for fire departments across the country. Other pressure-related products followed, the company's reputation grew, and the community prospered.

Jeffrey Kincaid, Jr., succeeded his father in 1995, and the business continued to grow — less rapidly but consistently. While not as inventive as his father, "Junior," as he was known to all, applied a steady hand, avoiding any risky product diversifications.

As a company, Kincaid wasn't flashy. But it had its niche and within that niche, no manufacturer was more respected.

Then came a huge shock which, about six months later, led to another of gigantic proportion.

Junior Kincaid drowned while on a fishing trip in Alaska. Word of his death was a gut punch to the town, employees, and their families. He was only 55, looked 15 years younger, and was widely respected.

Because everyone assumed Junior would continue to run the company for another ten or fifteen years, little thought had been given to succession planning.

Son Russell was next in line. But Junior and his team of managers were concerned the young man might not be up to the job. The suddenness of Junior's death, however, decided the issue. Kincaid Fabricators, after all, was a family-owned business. Ready or not, Russell, age 31, inherited the job.

The day after Junior's funeral, Russell abruptly moved into his father's office, bringing with him his attractive, well-endowed but modestly-skilled young secretary, Elise Fortney, and demoting Junior's long-time executive assistant, Florence Treadwell, to a job in accounts payable.

Although it was something of a given Russell eventually would take command, the aggressiveness with which he moved and the way he brutally dumped the loyal and experienced "Miss Florence", as most everyone addressed her, should have served as warning signs. The widely-held view was that she was as close to being indispensable as anyone in the company. "Miss Florence could damn-well run the company," was a phrase heard more than a few times over the years.

Russell lacked both the inventiveness of his grandfather and the business acumen of his father even though he had, at a leisurely pace, earned an MBA degree. He'd worked for a few years in sales and quality control, but now, as the third generation Kincaid, he was in charge.

His actions upon taking over caused unrest among employees. But, at first, they tended to rationalize them as the acts of an insecure young man believing he needed to demonstrate strength and authority. Their hope was that, over time, he'd grow into the job, gain confidence, and at least see the wisdom of relying on others for guidance.

However, with the passage of six or so months, it became clear he didn't want help. He neither sought nor appreciated advice. Most often, it was his way or the highway. The open-door policy his grandfather and father practiced, where anyone could drop in unannounced with a complaint, suggestion, or a simple "hello", changed overnight. Now, when Russell was in the office, the door was shut and Elise Fortney became the gate keeper, controlling who got in to see "the boss".

Russell seemed not to care all that much about the business his grandfather had founded and his father had managed. Other things, including the bright lights and social life of big cities and the physical attributes of Elise and other women, dominated his attention.

It was no secret Russell was a womanizer. Most everyone knew it. Secrets are hard to keep in a small town. His philandering had cost him his marriage. Beverly's filing for divorce several years earlier had been the talk of the town, and the back-and-forth was both ugly and very public.

Still, no one could have anticipated what was about to happen.

There had been rumors something, no one seemed to know what, was in the works. Out-of-towners no one knew were showing up at the plant and being quickly ushered into Russell's office. Speculation ran the gamut. Maybe Russell was hiring someone from the outside to handle the day-to-day part of his job; or maybe he was considering acquiring some related business (his father had explored a few such prospects in the past).

Then came the news. Russell was cashing out, selling Kincaid to Allied Manufacturing, a relatively new entry into the heavy valve-making business, based in Cleveland.

Allied had made overtures to Junior Kincaid a year before but was rebuffed. Now, with Junior out of the picture, they wasted no time in contacting Russell. At first, Russell was a bit leery. But, as the talks continued and Russell realized what was in it for him, he signed on to the deal.

The announcement came in the form of a short, to-the-point letter from Russell — not an in-person presentation. No introduction of the new owner beyond the name of the company. No reassurance to employees. No indication of Russell's or anyone else's role going forward. Just a closing line thanking everyone and wishing them well.

Nervousness immediately turned to disbelief.

Plant Manager Jacob (Jake) Walter, one of only two managers who reported directly to Russell, was as much in the dark as everybody else. Employees shut down their machines and twenty-five or so crowded around the door to his office.

"What the hell is going on?" they wanted to know.

Jake, obviously upset, could only reply, "All I know is we, apparently, have a new owner. I'll let you know when I learn anything more."

"You had to know this was in the works, didn't you?" a maintenance foreman asked.

Respected as a straight shooter, Jake replied, "Nope. Now go back to work. We've got some product to move out the door."

CHAPTER 3

All of Waterford was in a state of shock — hoping for the best but fearing the worst.

The worst came on Monday, December 11, four days after the initial letter. Kincaid Fabricators, a fixture in Waterford for over 50 years, was being shut down. A printed "Notice to Employees" said all of the company's equipment would be dismantled and moved to Cleveland. Employees with ten or more years of seniority would receive three months' severance; those with at least five would get two months', those with less than five but more than one, one month, and those with less than one, two weeks. No employees would be offered the option of moving to Cleveland to work for Allied.

"Kincaid operations will be shut down immediately," the notice stated. "Employees should clear out their desks/lockers and turn in their badges by end of shift today, December 11, 2016. Allied representatives are on site to facilitate the closure. Removal and relocation of machinery, equipment, and inventory will begin next week."

Then came the closing line: "The decision to centralize all manufacturing operations in Cleveland was difficult but necessary. We appreciate your service to Kincaid Fabricators and wish you well."

"Wish us well?" Jake Walter muttered as he read the notice aloud to several co-workers in his office. "Yeah, and don't let the door handle hit you in the ass on your way out."

Always the epitome of grace and professionalism, Miss Florence, standing alongside Jake, lost it. "That little shit," referring to Russell, "his father and grandfather must be turning over in their graves. I knew he was up to no good; I just didn't know what it was. Oh," she added, "and isn't the timing wonderful, two weeks before Christmas."

It was only a matter of minutes before what seemed like everyone in Waterford heard the news. How could this be happening? The company was successful. What would happen to Waterford? Would it become like so many West Virginia towns that lost their economic base, their way of life, their future?

People felt betrayed, and they knew who betrayed them — Russell Kincaid. He'd taken the money and run. This wasn't "just another company." This was "their company." It was their efforts and the efforts of those before them that had made it successful. It was as if someone had snatched the heart from their body. What kind of person would do this? Russell Kincaid had pocketed the fruit of their labor, stomped on the Kincaid family name, and didn't even have the guts to be on site to communicate his decision.

"That son-of-a-bitch" became the phrase most often heard that day and in the weeks that followed.

Waterford's weekly newspaper, "The Valley Beacon," normally published on Wednesdays, but long-time

Justifiable

Editor/Owner Bill Price, Reporter Donna Reynolds, and Press Operator Rufus Alexander worked through the afternoon and night to produce a four-page Special Edition the next day, Saturday, the 12th. The banner headline read: "Kincaid Shuts Down" followed by a sub-head, "All Employees Terminated."

The normal Saturday activity of folks doing their banking and shopping transformed into mini-town-hall-type gatherings as people shared their concerns, fears, and, without exception, anger.

Steve Insley, owner of Valley Hardware, and, for the last three years, Waterford's mayor, called an emergency meeting of the Town Council for Saturday morning. They agreed to see if there was anything their Congressman, Jay Bosworth, could do. Any violation of law, any way the transaction could be disallowed? Weren't employees and the community at least entitled to some advance notice?

Insley, known for his mild-manner, agreed to try to contact Russell and, as soon as possible, whomever was in charge at Allied in Cleveland.

The community deserved some answers.

"Damn it," Insley said, "any business is only as good as the people who work there. If Kincaid's worth buying, why the hell close down the plant? Why not keep it right here. Why not keep the people who know how to run it? It's the craziest thing I ever heard of," he said, shaking his head and raising up from his chair.

Turning to Police Chief Frank Wharton, Insley said, "Frank, there's gonna be some drinking tonight, so you'll want to staff up just in case some folks get a little rambunctious."

"Got it covered," Wharton replied, "though I'd rather go looking for Russell and lock him up on some trumped-up charge. Don't quote me."

Jake Walter, who had been plant manager for a dozen years, hated the prospect of seeking another job, but he'd have to. The one which was allowing him to send his daughter off to Ohio State and his son, who would graduate high school this coming year, to WVU in the fall, no longer existed. Jake was 57 and Waterford was home. Hell, he was born 30 miles from the plant.

But chances were dim he'd be able to find the kind of job somewhere in the area that would allow him to keep those promises to his children. Much as he hated the thought, he'd likely have to look elsewhere. He'd also have to face the possibility it might take some time to find someone interested in hiring a guy in his mid- to late- 50s.

CHAPTER 4

Darlene's Dream Diner had been a fixture in Waterford for more than a quarter century. The combination of a gregarious owner, delicious comfort food, and, yes, an African Grey parrot named Dagwood, who charmed and greeted every arriving customer with a "Hi, darlin'" explained why.

Ella Mae Gurney, Wally Hitchcock, and Phil Sweeney had made meeting for breakfast at Darlene's a Saturday morning tradition. All three worked in the casting department at Kincaid, Ella Mae for 19 years, Wally for 15, and Phil, "the youngster", for 11.

Normally they'd talk about the opening of deer hunting season, or fishing conditions in the Maplethorn, or Pastor So-and-So being chased out of town for "romantic improprieties". Sometimes, the conversation would stray into state or national politics but not too often because they all thought about the same. Democrats could do more to help working folks, they agreed, but voting Republican was out of the question.

This Saturday, as Phil slid into the booth already occupied by Ella Mae and Wally, Ella Mae, never one to mince her words, was the first to open up.

"That bastard. If ammunition wasn't so expensive, I'd go find Russell and shoot him, first in the ass and, after watching him scream and squirm for a few minutes, blow his friggin' head off."

"Well, good morning," Phil said, forcing a smile. "I guess you've already set the agenda."

Wally, always the most reasonable and steady of the three, stirred a second spoonful of sugar in his coffee. "You know what? We should have listened to those guys from the union back when they tried to get us to organize. Maybe if we were union, our jobs would have been protected. And maybe being union would have discouraged folks from buying us. We were too damn trusting. We assumed whichever one of the Kincaids was in charge would take care of us." He paused to take a sip. "God, I wish it was Russell who drowned instead of his daddy."

"Maybe that's the way I'll kill Russell," Ella Mae volunteered. "He'd suffer just about as much and it'd save the cost of ammo."

Phil rolled his eyes, something he did often enough that Ella Mae said just looking at him made her dizzy.

Wally always ordered three eggs over easy with country ham and a biscuit. This morning he wouldn't. Outwardly, he seemed calm enough, but his stomach was churning.

What would he and the others do? Hell, he'd just bought a fully-loaded, 4 x 4 Chevy pickup for which he'd stretched the payments out five years. Now he wished he'd gone to college rather than to Kincaid straight out of high school. The national economy wasn't all that good now, and West Virginia ... hell, it always seemed to be struggling. Not a great time to be looking for work.

"The kind of jobs we have — excuse me — had," Wally said, "are few and far between. It's all high tech nowadays. Shit, the little bit I know about computers I've learned from my son."

"You got that right," Ella Mae added, "look around in this room. We know most everyone here. And, unless I'm missing someone, I don't see any college whiz-kid graduates."

None of the three had their usual appetite. The shock and anger had taken care of that. However, Ella Mae managed to polish off a cinnamon roll the size of her face.

"Well," Phil said, "we'll all get paid for several months, and I'll be damned if I'm gonna let this ruin my kids' Christmas."

"Damn, Phil," Ella Mae said, reaching over to put her hands around his neck, "you're such a damn optimist."

With that, Wally asked, "Are we adjourned?"

"Yep," Ella Mae said, "I've gotta go home and kick the dog."

"How about breakfast on Tuesday?" Phil asked, smiling at Ella Mae's latest. "We've all got the day off."

"The first of many, unfortunately," Wally said, "but, yeah."

These were sturdy folks. West Virginians are. Anyone who knows anything about them knows that. They're survivors.

Out the three of them went, nodding and saying "see ya" to friends in Darlene's, each wondering what the future held, a little bit scared, and a lot mad. Even Dagwood's "Bye, darlin'" didn't have its usual cheering effect.

CHAPTER 5

More than a few old-timers openly cried as the Kincaid sign came crashing down, scattering glass and steel in its wake. It had been a landmark, the illuminated, yellow block letters having weathered severe, near-tornado winds several times over the years. Even more than a landmark, the sign had served as a reminder of stability and pride in knowing the products produced within those walls extinguished fires and saved countless lives.

Cranes lifted casting equipment weighing multiple tons out the loading bays onto flatbeds for transport by road or rail to Cleveland. The same for finishing mills, presses, saws, and every last machine tool. With few exceptions, the naked shell of the building was all that would be left. Former employees weren't allowed on the property; they could only watch from beyond the fence, and many did.

Miles Thompson, who'd retired 24 years earlier when he turned 65, leaned on his hickory cane, bowed his head, and said to no one in particular, "Never thought I'd see this. I put in 28 years, all of 'em right over there in packaging and shipping. This is the most depressing thing I've ever seen." He turned, shook his head, and slowly made his way across the street, stopping long enough to mutter to another onlooker, "I can't watch no more."

Chief Wharton had feared there might be some violence as folks saw a part of their lives torn apart, so he had his own force of five plus six state troopers at the ready in his department a block down Cedar Street.

The crews doing the dismantling were from out of state. They had no attachment to any of this. To them, it was just a job. Still, Wharton had to be prepared. Violence, especially by and against unions in the coal mining regions, was an ugly scar on West Virginia's past. Thankfully, the tension and uneasiness this day was limited to a few words here and there between the dismantling crews and just-terminated employees. Anger was still raw, but for now it had been mostly displaced by numbing sadness.

It might take a couple of weeks to finish all the removals, but Wharton was relieved. The first day was the one that worried him the most. He'd stay prepared; the troopers would come up from West Charleston each day, just in case. But for now, at least, the town had dodged a bullet.

Christmas was a welcome distraction. However, this year the mood was different. Most everyone in town was religious and much of the socializing was tied to church activities. Try as they might, folks couldn't help talking about the Kincaid fiasco. More than a few folks said they were looking for some Biblical justification to kill Russell Kincaid.

Sermons were devoted to surviving the tough times, to loving and helping each other, to the joy of charity, and the power of prayer. But not a single preacher dared mention forgiveness.

Now that they didn't have a job to report to, Ella Mae, Wally and Phil had increased the frequency of their breakfasts at Darlene's. The Saturday routine had expanded to add Tuesdays and Thursdays.

While most folks tried hard to put on a brave front, everyone knew everyone else shared their fear, and just being with others and talking things through helped them cope.

Normally talkative and upbeat, Phil had become less outgoing. "I've got to get my ass in gear and find something — anything — that'll pay the bills. We don't have any savings to speak of, and I can sure forget about making money on the sale of my house." He smiled and shook his head, "Hell, I wouldn't get enough to cover what I owe."

"You don't have to worry about that, Philly Boy," Wally said, "who'll still be around to buy a house?"

"Hey," Ella Mae said, "what makes you two hillbillies so sure someone won't come into town and put another business in our building?"

"Look around the state," Wally replied. "Do you see a lot of companies lining up to locate in our beloved Mountain State?"

"I hear you," she said, "but damn it, we got a great location, skilled people, good schools, and — at least for now — non-union. Don't give up so easy."

Wally didn't always agree with Ella Mae, but he appreciated this tough woman's optimism. God how he hoped some way, somehow, she was right. Whatever, he was going to do everything he could to continue to live in Waterford. There had to be something in Charleston or Parkersburg or across the river in Ohio. He'd been spoiled by his five-minute commute but he could deal with greater distances. He figured he needed to work another ten or fifteen years before considering retirement.

With breakfast now on the table, there was a momentary pause in the conversation. But only momentary.

Without any warning, Ella Mae sprung up out of the booth and clanged her knife against her water glass repeatedly to get others in Darlene's to listen up. "Raise your hands," she directed in her loud, gravelly voice, "if you agree we ought to find where that sniveling Russell Kincaid is holed up, drag him out, and shoot him."

Momentarily surprised by the outburst, hands then shot up, accompanied by hooting and hollering.

"Thank you, thank you," Ella Mae responded, turning from side to side and bowing. "Maybe we ought to get one of those television talking heads to come out here and take an opinion poll. I'll bet 'shoot the s.o.b.' would win by a landslide."

She sat back down to continued cheering, clearly satisfied with the affirmation.

"Jeez, Ella Mae," Wally said, knowing she was just letting off steam and, in the process, enjoying herself, "you'll be a prime suspect if anything happens to that lovely boy."

"That's okay, you get three squares a day at Moundsville, and I've heard the food isn't all that bad. And, hell, I'd die of old age before they got around to executing me."

CHAPTER 6

With the holidays over, unrest in Waterford grew. Increasingly, people were on edge. By now, most employees had filed for unemployment and some few had already received a first check. But, while anything was better than nothing, the amount was far short of what they'd been bringing home from Kincaid.

Then there was "the pride thing." These people were used to working hard, earning a wage, providing for their families. Being paid while not working had a bit of a sour taste of "welfare" attached to it. They knew they were entitled to it, and no one was turning it down, but somehow taking the payment diminished their pride and self image.

Most folks had begun doing all they could to make their severance pay stretch. Winter isn't the time for yard sales, but hand-lettered signs advertising everything from riding mowers to televisions and outboard motors decorated numerous front yards.

Word spread that Russell Kincaid had moved to Cleveland and had some kind of consulting agreement with Allied. That served to further intensify the hatred felt toward him. Not only had he pocketed millions from the sale (no one locally knew how much), but now he had a cushy job while everyone back in Waterford suffered.

Januarys often were bitterly cold as the temperature dropped, sometimes to single digits, and the winds swept across the river. Some years the Maplethorn even froze over. But this January had been mild and more of the same was predicted for early February.

The forecast for Wednesday, February 1, was broken clouds, a high of 48 degrees and a nighttime low of 34.

Joshua Harris, who washed dishes at Darlene's and rented a room above the Elk's hall, was walking the five blocks to work. It was 6 a.m. and his shift started in a half hour. He liked walking along the river, sometimes poking at a particular cluster of debris to see if there might be something of value hidden within. He also liked watching the mist rise slowly above the water.

This morning, just as he was passing Wilkens Ferry Landing which, before an up-river bridge was built some years ago, had provided small-barge river crossings, he noticed what at first looked like a large, whitish, plastic bag, inflated but partially submerged. It was about fifteen feet off shore. Curious, he walked closer to the river"s edge.

What he saw caused him to lose his breath. "Good God," he hollered, though no one was around to hear him. A chill ran up his spine. He paused for a moment, re-focusing his eyes to be sure he saw what he thought he saw. Then he took off running the remaining three blocks to Darlene's

Running through the door, he nearly knocked Darlene over. Dagwood the parrot barely had time to do his "Hi, darlin'".

"Josh, what the hell ..."

By then, Josh was breathless and shaking all over. "Miss Darlene. Th ... th ... th ... there's a dead person in the river."

"What are you talking about, Josh?"

"I'm saying, Miss Darlene, I just saw a body in the river, down by Wilkens Landing."

Any doubt Darlene may have had disappeared.

"Okay, Josh, sit down. I'll call the police. You just sit here," motioning to a chair that normally was used by customers waiting for take-out orders.

Unable to control his shaking, Josh did as he was told.

The phone rang twice. "Police Department ..."

"Molly? This is Darlene. Is Frank there?"

"Oh, hi. Yes, he just walked in. Are you okay?"

"Yeah, but I need to talk to him right away."

"Chief, Darlene needs to speak with you."

Frank Wharton loved Waterford. It was home, and he felt a responsibility to do what he could to keep it safe. He made a practice of getting into the office early because he liked having what, usually, was a quiet time to catch up on any leftover details and organize his day.

Not today.

No more than ten minutes after hanging up, he and Deputy Chief Elmer Johnson had picked Josh up at Darlene's and were at Wilkens Landing.

The naked body had washed up closer to the embankment, so with just a step or two into the shallow water, Frank and Elmer were able to tug it ashore.

The body had been face down, but they'd already determined it was a male.

"Help me turn him over," Frank said to Elmer.

"Oh, my Lord, my Lord." Frank repeated. "You know who this is?"

Elmer bent over a bit closer.

"Is it Russell ...?"

Frank didn't let him finish. "Damn right, it's Russell Kincaid."

They both raised up.

"Jesus, Mary, and Joseph, what a way to start the day." No sooner had Frank said those words than he bent back over and stared at Russell's head.

"And he didn't drown, Elmer. See this hole over here close to his ear?" Frank said, pointing his pen. "See it? He was shot."

"Yep, sure looks like it."

"Elmer, don't touch anything. I'll drive Josh back to Darlene's, make some phone calls, and try to be back within a half hour. We'll want to tape this area off, so you might want to get started on it."

"Check. See you then."

Darlene saw the chief's car pull up and went out to meet Frank and Josh.

"Here," Frank said, opening the passenger side door, "get in. I need to talk to you and Josh, who was still in the back seat, for a minute.

He took a deep breath. "I'm gonna tell you something you can't tell anyone else. This is very important. Don't tell anybody. That clear?"

"Yes," they replied in unison.

"The body is a young man. He didn't drown; he's been shot. Elmer's down at the river taping off the scene, so word is gonna get out. You know this town. People talk. Rumors spread like wildfire — especially now after the Kincaid closure."

"Don't confirm anything to anybody. You know nothing." He stared directly at Josh. "There will be a time when I have to disclose you discovered the body, Josh, but not now."

"Yes, sir," Josh said, no longer shaking but listening intently to every word.

"One other thing. We know who the victim is. Josh knows because he heard it from Elmer and me. It's Russell Kincaid."

"Mother of God!" Darlene said, eyes bulging as she cupped both hands over her mouth, where they remained for a few seconds.

"This is really important," Frank said. "Do not ... do not either of you say anything about Russell Kincaid. I don't want anything to get in the way of my investigation. As I said, rumors will fly, people will come up with anything and everything. But I need you two to be dumb."

"That's not hard for me," Darlene said, briefly regaining her legendary good humor.

"Me, either, Chief Wharton," Josh said. "Can I go to the kitchen now? Those dirty dishes are going to begin piling up."

"Wait a minute, Josh," Darlene said. "I'm sure those few customers here this morning saw Frank picking you up. And, maybe one or two saw me walking out and getting in the car. How do we handle that, Frank?"

Frank thought for a few seconds, "Just tell them to enjoy their breakfast and walk away. I need to buy a little time. I'll tell you when you can speak up and what you can say."

"Another day in almost heaven, West Virginia," Darlene chuckled as she and Josh exited the car and headed into the diner. She knew it was un-Christian-like to celebrate a murder. But, Russell Kincaid's? She had to fight back the urge to dance.

CHAPTER 7

Elmer decided to hold off striping the scene until Frank returned. "Five or six people drove by, stopped and asked me what I was looking for. I lied, put my phone to my ear, and told 'em I was just taking a short break. The river bank blocked their view enough, so none of 'em could see the body. I figured if I strung the tape they'd know something was up and hightail it over."

"Good thinking," Frank said, remembering why he had chosen Elmer two years earlier to be Deputy Chief.

Now, however, Frank had brought two additional cops and the fire department's ambulance with him, so passersby would know something serious had happened.

"Billings," Frank called out to Patrolman Joe Billings, "get out on the street and direct traffic. Keep it moving. I don't want anyone pulling over and gawking."

Frank directed the two fire department EMTs to the body. "Fellas, take him straight to the coroner's in Charleston. No talking to anyone else. I've already told them you're coming. Here, back your vehicle up as close as you can to the bank. I don't want people to see what's going on."

"Gotcha, boss."

"Oh, shit, is that who I think it is?" EMT Joe Smiley asked as he began positioning the victim in the body bag.

"Yeah," Frank said. "But I'm gonna be all over your ass if I learn you spread the word. Understand?"

"Yes, sir," Smiley said, saluting respectfully.

With the ambulance now pulling away, Frank turned again to Elmer. "On second thought, I don't think there's any point in taping this area off. You can look around a bit, but I wouldn't hang out for too long. Nothing happened here. He drifted down the river. No question about that. Keep Billings on the road while you're here. Then bring him back with you. We got a lotta work ahead of us."

Driving the five blocks back to his office, Frank went over in his mind some of the things he needed to do. First, he'd phone State Police Superintendent Don Blackford. He'd work closely with Blackford, and provide whatever support he could. But this was going to be big. Really big. The state would take the lead.

After he talked to Don, a good friend who years before was a classmate at the Police Academy, he'd try to get in touch with Kincaid's ex-wife, Beverly. Meantime, he might have to confirm to the media that a body had been found, but he wasn't about to identify who it was until after he reached her. Then, unless events overtook his best intentions, he'd try to chase down Russell's secretary, Elise Fortney. The word was that she and Russell were living together somewhere on the outskirts of Cleveland. Someone at Allied Manufacturing should know.

Molly Bevans, who had worked as dispatcher at the police department since graduating high school 10 years earlier, knew better than to question Chief Wharton when he swept by her work station.

He closed his office door and then, as quickly, opened it. "Molly, I've got to make a couple of calls, so don't put anybody through to me. I'll bring you up to speed as soon as I can."

"Yes, sir," she said. She loved the excitement of her job and she loved working for Frank Wharton and the team he'd built. They were a small department. But they knew what they were doing. They took good care of Waterford.

Frank decided to call Superintendent Don Blackford's private cell phone number. It was only a few minutes past seven and he figured Don would still be at home.

"Hey, top of the morning to you, Frank," Blackford answered. "What's up?"

"I've got a murder. You got a minute?"

"Yep, for you and for a murder, I've got as much time as you need."

Frank briefly covered all that had occurred in the previous hour, ending with, "This is gonna be big, Don, because the victim is Russell Kincaid, the most hated person in Waterford."

"I'll be damn. Somebody got to him." Blackford was well aware of the sudden closure of the plant and the termination of everyone who worked there.

"Yep, and as soon as the word gets out, there'll be dancing in the streets and the media circus will begin. The body is on its way to the coroner's. He should be there by the time you get to your office. Looks like a single bullet shot to the head. Your guy will be able to give us an idea of how long he was in the river, but I'm thinking not too long because I couldn't see any decomposition."

"Okay," Don said, "I know you have other calls to make. I'll send Spence Atkins and some of my guys from homicide out your way. They should be there within the hour. We'll refer media to you for now. Let me know when you reach his ex. Meantime, no confirmation of identity, right?"

"Yeah. We're on the same page. And it will be good to see Spence, even under the circumstances."

"Yeah, he's the best," Don said. "I guess I don't have to worry about planning my day, old pal."

"Me either," Frank replied.

Normally fairly laid back, Frank could feel the adrenalin pumping. He had put on some weight in recent years but, with time spent in the gym, kept himself in good shape. Years before, he had declined an opportunity to join the Charleston police department and even considered an offer from Cincinnati. Both would have paid more and either might have led to substantial promotions over the years. But both would have meant dealing with a lot more criminal activity. And, with that, more pressure; less time for family. Waterford was peaceful. It was where he felt most comfortable, where for the most part he was his own boss.

So much for being peaceful, he thought after ending the call.

CHAPTER 8

Beverly Kincaid continued to live in the house she and Russell had built six years earlier. Now, she lived there alone, having claimed the house as part of the settlement of their highly contentious divorce.

They had been high school sweethearts, continued their romance through four years at West Virginia University, and married upon graduation. At first, any problems were kept from public view but then things exploded.

Word spread that Russell was bedding young women from Charleston to Parkersburg. His "afternoon breaks" from work and "late-night meetings" up and down the state became well known.

Beverly put up with his infidelity as long as she could. Then her anger went off the charts, culminating with the "Honk if you've been screwed by Russell Kincaid" bumper sticker she stuck to the back of her BMW.

The divorce had been final for more than two years when Frank knocked on her door that February morning.

"Who is it," came the voice from inside.

"It's Frank Wharton, Beverly. Sorry for not calling ahead, but I need to talk with you."

"Just a minute, Frank."

Still in her robe, Beverly led Frank into the breakfast room.

"Want some coffee? I just made it."

"Sure, thanks," Frank said, reminded that the pace of the morning hadn't allowed time for his normal caffeine fix.

Beverly placed the two mugs, hers and his, on the table and sat down.

"Okay, Frank, what's he done now?"

Frank paused. This was the part of his job he disliked the most. Telling anyone about the death of a family member never got easier.

"Beverly. I am so sorry. Russell is dead. We ..."

"Dead?" Beverly interrupted. "How?"

"We found his body in the river down by Wilkens Ferry Landing this morning."

"In the river? You're telling me he drowned?"

"No, he was shot," Frank had been carefully observing Beverly's expressions as she asked questions and he replied.

He expected she would show shock. She didn't. Once the divorce was final, she had withdrawn from the community, preferring instead long-established friendships in Charleston and across the river in Ohio. He knew she continued to despise the man who'd cheated on her, but she had loved him for a number of years earlier. He thought there might be a tear or two, some indication of sorrow.

She looked down at her coffee. Her hand holding the mug was steady. No shaking. No sign of nervousness or sadness. Then, after a pause, "Do you know who did it?"

"No. We just discovered him a couple of hours ago. I'm going to have to disclose his identity," Frank said. "But I wanted to tell you first."

Still dry-eyed and steady, Beverly replied, "I appreciate that. I'll give you my cell phone number so you can reach me if you need to. I'm not going to answer the house phone."

"Good idea. Now, one more thing." This, too, was a requirement Frank dreaded. "I need you to confirm it's Russell. It is. I'm sure. But we need your confirmation. We can do this either of two ways. I can have you driven to the coroner's or, if you'd rather, I can show you a couple of photos on my phone. Either way works but, I warn you, his body was in the water for a while so there's been some bloating and discoloration."

There was no hesitation. "Show me the pictures."

At this point, Beverly did take a deep breath. "It's him, Frank. I don't need to see anything more."

"Again, I am sorry to be the bearer of bad news ..."

"That's okay, he lived the life he wanted to live, took the risks he wanted to take."

Walking to his car, Frank hashed over in his mind the reaction he'd just witnessed. He'd need additional time to try to figure it out. He'd share Beverly's reaction with Don Blackford and Spence Atkins. And he knew Spence would have additional questions for her.

Now he would try to reach Elise Fortney, Russell's "secretary."

He thought it might be a bit difficult because he wasn't sure she worked for Russell in his consulting capacity at Allied. It turned out to be easy. Using Allied's general office number in Cleveland he asked to be connected to Russell's office.

"Mr. Kincaid's office ... this is Elise."

Frank had met Elise once or twice when she was at Kincaid Fabricators. "Is this Elise Fortney?"

"Yes, sir, may I ask who's calling?"

Frank reintroduced himself and relayed the news.

"Oh, no. Oh, no," followed by what seemed like a couple of minutes of sobbing.

Then "where ... how?"

Frank answered without any elaboration.

Elise continued to sob. "Oh, God. That poor man. I bet it was some awful person back there. You know they hated him. He was afraid something like this would happen."

"Did he receive any threats?"

"Yes."

Frank didn't want to get into too much depth with this initial call, but he did want to establish some kind of record so what Elise said now could be compared to what she might say later.

"What kind of threats?"

"He didn't say. He just said he got them."

"Did he report them to the police?"

"I told him to," she said, her voice clearing, "but I don't know."

"Did you get any?"

"No, but I don't answer our home phone unless I can see the number and know who's calling."

Frank made a note. "Our home phone" ... that confirmed they were living together.

"When did you last see Russell?"

"The day before yesterday."

"What time?"

"About three or four."

"Not since then?"

"No, he had to go to Charleston for some meetings."

"Did you and he talk since then."

"No."

Frank chose not to ask any more questions. He'd promptly share what Elise had said with Spence or Don.

Among the things they'd need to know was where the murder had been committed. Was it Cleveland? Waterford? Somewhere in between? The coroner ought to be able to come up with a fairly precise estimate of the time of death. Knowing that would help.

Was this a revenge killing related to the shutdown? If so, the possible suspects numbered in the hundreds. Conversations overheard in Darlene's or the grocery store or even at after-church socials were replete with hatred toward Russell. Had this rage driven someone or some group to murder him? Or was his death the consequence of Russell's sexual escapades. For now, only questions, no answers.

Frank phoned Don Blackford to fill him in on his conversations with Beverly and Elise.

"My homicide guys will be talking with them later today, tomorrow at the latest,"

Don said. "The coroner is working on the body now. I'll let you know what he comes up with. I've already talked to homicide in Cleveland, and we'll talk more later today.

"You still want me to deal with the initial media?" Frank asked.

"Yes. Just the basics, though: name, when and where found, and under investigation by the State as a possible homicide. Then give them our number. We'll handle it after your initial confirmation."

CHAPTER 9

No sooner had Frank hung up than Molly told him Bill Price had phoned and needed to talk with him.

"I just knew he couldn't give me a few minutes to catch my breath," Frank responded, simultaneously punching in the Valley Beacon's phone number which he'd memorized years before.

"I just heard Russell Kincaid's been murdered. What can you tell me?"

Frank and Bill had been friends for years and enjoyed kidding each other. So, Frank was tempted to respond, "Oh, you mean that old story?" But now wasn't the time for kidding.

He took Bill through what he knew except for the conversations he'd had with Beverly and Elise. No elaboration; just the facts.

Bill knew better than to press his friend. He knew Frank would tell him what he could, but he knew he had more pressing things to do than talking to the press.

Minutes later came the expected call from the Charleston Gazette-Mail, followed a half-hour later by the Parkersburg News.

By then, Spence Atkins, Don Blackford's homicide chief, had arrived and he and Frank scheduled a press conference for 1 p.m. Neither would go beyond what Frank had already said except for Spence adding that his office, while taking the lead, would be working closely with Frank and with the police in Cleveland.

Word spread like crazy through Waterford. The locals had been through so much, and now this. Those who a short time before had lost their jobs were either jubilant or, at least, satisfied. Most felt Russell got what he deserved, what they themselves would have done if they'd thought they could get away with it.

No one, not even the most God-fearing, expressed regret. Speculation was all over the lot, but most felt someone in Waterford must have done it. "Vigilante justice," as one put it.

Ella Mae, Wally and Phil agreed revenge was most likely.

"You can tell me," Ella Mae said, leaning across the booth and lowering her raspy voice to a whisper, "I promise I'll never tell. You two blockheads do it?"

"Not me," Wally said, raising his hands in surrender. "I'm not smart enough to get away with it."

"Don't be looking at me, pretty lady," Phil said. "I'm not that good a shot."

"You're pretty damn good with a rifle," Wally countered while pointing at Ella Mae. "I'm thinking you might have done it."

"You just keep thinking that, mister," she responded, turning her attention to the sweet roll in front of her. "I ain't sayin'."

"Do either of you feel just a little bit guilty being so happy?" Wally asked.

Phil shook his head.

As Wally expected, Ella Mae was expansive. "I haven't been this happy since I divorced Sam 15 years ago. From now on, this day should be a God damn state holiday. Maybe we ought to name it after Dagwood."

With that, Wally almost choked on his coffee. And Phil, as usual, just rolled his eyes.

Dagwood heard his name. All parrots are smart. African Greys are among the smartest, and Dagwood was no exception. "Dagwood, Dagwood," he blurted out so loud it could be heard in the kitchen.

"Hush, pretty bird," Darlene said. "Pretty bird, pretty bird" came the squawked reply.

CHAPTER 10

Two days passed without any breakthrough. Spence had a lengthy visit with Beverly Kincaid. Having learned from Frank how ugly the divorce had been, he still wasn't fully prepared for how calmly she was taking Russell's murder. He continued to consider her a person of interest. But, you'd think a suspect would try to demonstrate innocence by showing how shocked and saddened she was. Beverly didn't make the effort.

The Cleveland police hadn't come up with anything. They had talked at length with Elise Fortney. She had reiterated her belief that someone in Waterford was responsible, but didn't have any names to suggest. She did say Russell didn't like Jake Walter, the plant manager, and that if he hadn't sold out he would have replaced him.

State troopers joined Waterford Patrolman Billings in searching both sides of the river bank upstream of town for any evidence. Nothing so far.

Spence set up shop in the office next to Frank's. He'd go back to Charleston each night but days were spent in Waterford. They established a routine. Eight a.m. every morning in Frank's office for a shared status report.

"You should be the one to talk initially with Jake Walter, " Spence said.

"Yeah, I know him pretty well. I can't see him as a suspect. But who knows? Jake loved the previous Kincaids, and maybe he knew Russell wanted him out."

Going down the list of "possibles" they hit next on Florence Treadwell. Spence said, "You go first on this one, too, and I'll follow up."

"I know this much," Frank said, "Miss Florence was plenty mad. First, for being demoted and, second, for the shutdown. That company, and the Kincaids prior to Russell, were like family to her."

Jake was in the garage working on an old Ford he was restoring when Frank drove up.

"Hey, Frank," he said, grabbing a cloth to wipe his hands. "What brings you here?"

"You got a couple of minutes?"

"Sure, come on in the house. You want some coffee or something?"

"Not a thing. I'm fine."

"How's your investigation going?"

"It's going. These things take time. I need to ask you a few questions."

"Fire away."

"How did you hit it off with Russell?"

Jake had thought Frank might ask him about others at the plant. He was taken aback by the question and paused for a couple of seconds before answering.

"We got along. He sure wasn't like his dad, though."

"Did you at any point think he wanted you out of the picture?"

Jake paused again. Where was Frank going with these questions? "I really hadn't thought of that. One thing I did know for sure, he needed people around him who knew how to run things, because he didn't."

"Would you be surprised if I told you someone told me Russell was going to let you go if he hadn't sold Kincaid?"

"Hey, people talk. They speculate. You know this town. Some folks knew I was frustrated. But, yes, I'd be surprised if he was thinking of firing me because, as I said, he needed me."

At this point, Jake was getting more than a little uneasy.

"Jake, I have to ask you, did you have anything to do with Russell's death?"

Jake didn't pause on this one. "No, Frank, nada, zilch, nothing."

"Do you have any idea who might have been sufficiently angry he'd kill him?"

"No. Everyone, and I mean everyone, was pissed off, that's for sure. But kill Russell? No, I can't think of anyone."

"The reason I ask is because you and Florence Treadwell are the only people who literally knew everybody at the plant."

Frank shuffled a few pages in his pocket-sized notebook, "Jake, where were you on January 30th and 31st?"

"I'm sure I was here all day, fiddling around with this wreck of a car. It takes my mind off other stuff. Vivian and I went to Darlene's for supper one of the nights; then straight home."

Neither Jake nor Frank said anything more for a minute as Frank made a few notes.

Jake couldn't take it any longer. "Frank, you're not really thinking I had anything to do with this, are you?"

"We've got to cover all the bases, Jake. I'm pretty sure there's only a handful of folks in town who want us to solve this one. But we've got a job to do. We've got to find out who did this. Thanks for your time. I'll be in touch if we have any more questions. Best to Vivian."

Jake watched as Frank drove down the gravel driveway, then walked back to the garage, picking up a wrench on his way and feeling a little queasy.

CHAPTER 11

Florence Treadwell, apparently with the exception of Russell Kincaid and maybe Elise Fortney, was universally liked and respected at the plant and, Frank knew, by non-company folks in the community.

Not only was she the fount of all information about the business, she found time to chair the Fletcher County Library Board, coordinate Waterford's semi-annual blood drives, and play the organ at the First United Methodist Church every Sunday.

Frank could only imagine how hurt she felt when young Russell shoved her aside and installed Elise in her place. But, she hadn't quit, though she certainly had the years of service to do so and live off the pension she'd earned.

Except for her initial, untypical "that little shit" response to Russell's selling the business and shutting down the plant, she had retained the poise and dignity for which she was known.

Among her many qualities, Frank had always been impressed with her intelligence. "Whip smart" was the best description.

Miss Florence never married. The Kincaids had been her "family." The feeling, up to the time Russell took charge, was mutual. Now 63 and gray-haired, she had retained her slender frame. Folks commented they never saw Miss Florence in jeans or, for that matter, slacks or shorts. Nope, dresses and skirts, and when at work or any place in public, heels.

Frank would pursue the same line of questioning he had with Jake Walter. Unlike with Jake, he'd phoned Miss Florence to set a time to meet. They agreed on 10 a.m. at her modest apartment, the one she'd moved to fifteen or twenty years before.

As expected, she was dressed in an age-appropriate blouse and skirt and, of course, heels.

"Hello, Frank. It's good to see you."

"Miss Florence, it's good to see you, too. How are you doing?"

"Come. Sit down. How about a nice hot cup of tea?"

"Yes, ma'am, thank you."

After a bit of small talk about the upcoming blood drive where Frank always donated and the unseasonably mild winter weather, Florence began.

"Oh, Frank, what's going to happen to our town? What's next? It makes me want to cry. These poor people."

That was just like Miss Florence: worried about the town, about others, not thinking about herself. What a class lady, Frank thought.

"We'll get through this," Frank said. "We're West-Virginia tough."

"Oh, Lord, I hope you're right. I couldn't in a million years think something like this could happen."

"Miss Florence, the State Police will want to talk with you. They have the lead on this. But, meantime, I need to ask you some questions." Frank flipped open his note pad.

"Ask anything you want, Frank."

"Do you know of anyone, anyone who might have been mad enough to kill Russell?"

"I've thought about that a lot," she said. "More tea?"

"No, thanks, I'm fine." Frank was anxious to hear her answer.

"You know, everyone was upset. Russell didn't have a lot of friends. He didn't want to listen to anyone. It's such a shame. Kincaid was a fine company, wonderful people, wonderful reputation. We were all in a state of shock when his father died. What a tragedy. Even though Russell was different from his father, everyone wanted him to succeed. It was in everyone's interest.

"But then," she paused, took a deep breath, "he threw it all away, everything his grandfather and father had built."

She hadn't answered Frank's question but he'd give her time.

"Tempers were quite hot. You can't blame folks. Their company and, for many, their life's work was being snatched away. To sell the business is bad enough, but to dismantle the plant and terminate everyone, it just makes me want to cry.

"I don't have any idea who might have killed Russell. And, as I said, I've given it some thought."

"Do you believe it was someone in the company?"

"I suppose that's most likely. But you know Russell couldn't keep his fly zipped. Maybe somebody somewhere else caught him in the act."

Frank showed a bit of surprise at the proper Miss Florence's description but not by her mentioning the possibility that Russell's philandering had caught up with him.

"What was the relationship between Russell and Jake Walter?"

"Oh, that wonderful man, Jake. What a jewel. He tried his best to work with Russell, but I think Russell somehow felt intimidated by Jake because Jake knew so much about the business and Russell, so little. Now, why would someone whose name is on the building, who owns the business, be intimidated by an employee? I don't understand it. But I think Russell was."

"Do you believe Jake could somehow be involved in Russell's death?"

"Oh, no. He was shattered by what Russell did. Shocked, mad ... we all were. But Jake having anything to do with Russell's death? No. Absolutely not."

Frank decided not to ask Florence where she was on January 30 and 31. Instead he asked, "When and how did you hear Russell had been killed?"

"Darlene phoned. At first, I couldn't believe it. But you know Darlene. She knows everything before anyone else knows anything."

They shared smiles at that truism. Darlene was a master at "breaking news" before there was social media or cable.

That reminded Frank. Darlene would be his next interview.

"What did Darlene say?"

"She said for me to not say anything. Then she told me; said Josh, her dishwasher, had found him."

"What time did she call?"

"It was early. Maybe 7 or 7:30, something like that."

So much for Darlene's commitment to keep a secret, Frank thought.

"Do you know if she called anyone else?"

"I don't know. Darlene and I have known each other for years. We talk a lot."

"I'm done, Miss Florence, thanks for the tea and your time."

"You're welcome, Frank. I'd like to wish you luck but if someone local did this, I wouldn't mind them getting away with it."

"I hear you. I'll call if I have any more questions."

CHAPTER 12

Mid-afternoon, between the lunch crowd and dinner, was the best time to talk with Darlene Davis, who was celebrating her 26th year of owning and operating Darlene's Dream Diner, considered the best place for comfort food for miles around. There was broad agreement Darlene's Southern fried chicken was the best ever, and her biscuits and pie, especially the fresh peach, were to die for. If all that wasn't enough, there was always Dagwood's "hi's" and "bye's." Where else in the world could a person go and enjoy this combination?

No one Frank knew was more down-to-earth than Darlene and no one had her finger on the pulse of Waterford like Darlene did.

She'd tried to keep her figure over the years, but her own good cooking had changed it to what she jokingly but descriptively called, husky. Her hairdo never changed over the years, always the same, a beehive with never a strand out of place.

She knew most customers by name, but for the men, chose "Hon." Children were either "Beautiful" or "Handsome." Women most often were accorded their given name.

Darlene was the personification of hard work done good naturedly. If anyone couldn't get along with her, the problem was theirs, not Darlene's. She also could be tough when the situation called for it, like when someone had a few too many beers and got verbally abusive. "Time to go home, Hon. Sleep tight," she'd say as she gently but efficiently guided the offender outside, often recruiting someone to drive him home.

Dagwood the parrot punctuated the friendliness of the diner. Darlene had acquired him soon after buying the place and right away posted a cautionary sign atop his cage that read: "Do Not Curse In Front of Dagwood." It had worked because Dagwood had not incorporated curse words in his ever-growing vocabulary.

To guarantee privacy, Frank had asked Darlene to come to his office.

"Hi, Hon, how you doing?"

Frank had looked forward to meeting with Darlene mainly because she "heard it all" at the diner. That's where people opened up, where they bragged, complained, argued, joked, cheered, you name it. He also liked her as a person and as someone who'd be straight with him.

"I'm busier than I'd like to be," he replied.

"I don't doubt it. I just wish we could call things even and get on with life. The guy who did everything he could to kill this town got himself killed."

"So, you're saying he deserved what he got?" Frank asked.

"Yes, sir. Justice. What goes around, comes around. An eye for an eye."

"Still, I've got a murder case to solve."

"I know you do, but I can still dream, can't I?"

"What are you hearing?"

"People are still pissed off. This bastard screwed up their lives. It's not like he had to do this. He already had plenty of money. He could take his little trips whenever he got bored. Hell, he could screw his way up and down the state and across the river. Why'd he have to mess up everybody else's life? He was a greedy little prick, that's why."

Darlene was warming up and Frank didn't interrupt.

"I don't know what kind of gun was used to shoot him, but practically every man and most boys over 14 here in Waterford have one, two, probably more. You know that, Frank. We don't play golf or tennis around here, we shoot. Hell, I've got a 45 I keep in the diner and two rifles and one 12 gauge at home. Gotta have my guns."

Frank knew locating the weapon would be a challenge. And, even if it was found, tying it to someone in town would be the longest of long shots.

"So, what are you hearing?" Frank persisted.

"Mostly it's along the lines of 'I would've shot him myself if I thought I could have got away with it'. That kind of stuff."

"You said, 'mostly'. What else?"

"Oh, some folks feel some sadness about Russell. But, so far, they're in the minority. And I think some of their sadness is about how this might reflect badly on our town."

"If you were in my shoes, who do you think you'd want to talk to?" Frank didn't remember ever asking this question in his years of interrogating.

"I don't know but I'll keep my ears open. Maybe someone will want to claim credit. Stranger things have happened. You'll be the first to know if I hear anything."

"Thanks. I'm gonna need all the help I can get."

After Darlene left, Frank leaned back, put his feet on his desk, closed his eyes and thought: Solving this is going to take someone overhearing someone else bragging or claiming he knows who did it. And the two best places for that to happen are Darlene's and the Roadside Bar, which was two blocks down the street.

It had been a long day. He'd see Augie Martino, the owner/barkeep at Roadside, tomorrow.

CHAPTER 13

Roadside Bar stayed open weeknights till eleven, so Frank asked Augie to come to his office in the morning. They decided on 9. Frank said he needed only an hour, and that would free Augie to open up before noon.

Augie had come to town four years earlier from up state, buying the bar from a long-time owner who retired and moved to Florida. Frank's officers had been called to the bar a number of times over the years, sometimes to prevent a fight, more likely to break one up.

Roadside wasn't a family place. It was as advertised: a bar. Walking in, the aroma was one of smoke and stale beer. Augie didn't get rich running the place, but he had a stable of "regulars." Food was limited to hot dogs, hamburgers, fries, and chili, if he felt like making it. And, of course, beer nuts.

Years before, to hear Augie tell it, he'd been a pretty good boxer; got to the finals of the Pennsylvania Golden Gloves Tournament before being knocked out. He drove delivery trucks for a dozen years, saved his money, and ended up buying Roadside on the cheap.

His middle-weight physique had morphed into a substantial pot belly over the years, but he could still take care of himself and called the cops only when he needed reinforcement.

He was on time for his meeting with Frank.

"Thanks for coming in, Augie."

"Yes, sir, Chief."

Frank went through the routine that he was working with the State Police on the investigation into Russell Kincaid's murder.

"Did Kincaid ever come in your bar?"

"Not often, but, yeah, maybe five or ten times. But not lately. I hadn't seen him for, I don't know, maybe six months."

"What kinds of things did you hear about Russell?"

"People didn't much like him even before he left town. Thought he was arrogant, full of himself."

"What about after he shut down the plant?"

"Guys were really pissed."

"Any threats?"

"Lots. Every damn night. But I took them as just threats."

"How can you be sure?" Frank asked.

"I guess I can't. But I've gotten to know most of these guys pretty well, and I think they were just jawing, letting off steam. They'd sometimes really get going with ridiculous stuff, like lynching him from that big oak in the park."

Frank reiterated that this was a crime most in the community didn't want solved, but that he had a job to do and needed the help of folks like Augie.

"Of the guys who come in, which ones do you think I should talk with."

Frank could see this question made Augie uncomfortable. He hesitated before answering. "I don't want this getting back to me, okay?"

"Absolutely," Frank assured.

Augie thought for a few seconds. "Maybe Albert Price, maybe Milt Bowman."

"Why them?"

"Both are hotheads; both are a little bit crazy."

"Anything special they said?"

"No, but they were always part of the back and forth; always mouthing off."

Frank made a note to check to see if either had a record.

"How often did Price and Bowman come?"

"Every night. I give them an 'A' for attendance. They're regulars."

"So you would remember if they weren't there?"

"Yes, sir. As I said, they were a little over the top in what they said, so I think I'd remember if they weren't there."

Frank would check them out and share their names with Spence.

"How's business since the plant closed?"

"It's slowed a bit. Maybe the wives are keeping their out-of-work husbands home. What I worry about is what happens when unemployment comp runs out. I hope this town doesn't just dry up. This bar doesn't make much, but it's all I got."

Augie promised to contact Frank if he heard anything that might be helpful.

CHAPTER 14

Frank and Spence Atkins agreed it was time to provide State Police Superintendent Don Blackford, Spence's boss, an update.

Frank went first, listing who he had interviewed, why he chose them, and what, if anything, he had learned.

Spence said he had talked with his counterparts at the Cleveland Police Department. So far, nothing from there. "I plan to follow up with most of those folks Frank has interviewed. Folks like Kincaid's secretary/girlfriend, Elise Fortney, Florence Treadwell, the owners of the diner and bar, managers at the plant. Then we can compare notes and see if there are any contradictions or new information."

"Any early impressions?" Don asked.

"Only that no one's sorry Russell's dead," Frank said, "but we already figured that would be the case."

"Are you pretty sure he was murdered because of what he did in selling the business?"

"I don't think we can say that yet," Spence said, looking at Frank, who nodded agreement. "We need to find and talk to some of Kincaid's sexual partners, and we need to talk more to his ex-wife, Beverly. She makes no secret of despising Russell."

"We haven't discounted the possibility he was shot for sleeping with someone and then tossed in our river to shift the blame," Frank said. "But I'll be surprised if that's the case. I think this one is home grown, an act of revenge."

"At this point," Spence said, "I think we can assume no one is going to rat out anyone. That is, unless we put up some reward money."

"I agree," Frank said. "We can't expect that kind of help. But maybe, just maybe because Russell's murder was so popular, someone will be tempted to claim credit. It'd probably have to be a slip of the tongue ... probably something said after too many beers or bourbon.

"I'm going to spend more time with Darlene, the diner owner, and Augie, the bar owner," Frank added. "Most likely, that's where that kind of talk might take place."

"Have either of you considered the possibility of a contract killing?" Don asked.

"That's always a possibility, boss," Spence said. "There, again, either someone needs to brag or be ratted out."

"And I guess there's no appetite locally to raise any reward money," Don said, pretty sure he already knew the answer.

"You got that right," Frank replied. "They don't want this thing solved. No one feels threatened by some killer running around looking for victims. They've concluded Russell was the sole intended target and, by the way, the intensity of hatred so many feel may damn-well increase when the severance money runs out and they don't have another job."

"I'll see if I can get the state to put up some reward money, but I doubt I'll be successful," Don said. "Money's always tight, but it's really tight at this five minutes, and

I expect no one will be interested in setting a go-it-alone precedent. You're sure the town won't ante up at least part?"

"Positive," Frank said.

"Spence is going to follow up with most of the people I've talked with, and my next visit will be with Robbie Brownell. He ran the sales and marketing side of the business. He and Jake Walter, the plant manager, were the only two who reported directly to Russell's father and then to Russell. Of course, Florence Treadwell reported to the father, but that changed in a hurry when Russell took over."

"What about personnel actions?" Don asked. "Any recent firings or demotions other than Miss Treadwell?"

"Good point," Frank said. "We're gonna dig into that. And I'm not gonna ignore retirees, folks who spent a career working for the Kincaids."

"Okay, gentlemen," Don concluded. "Keep me posted. This one's not going to be easy. We're going to need some help, not to mention luck."

CHAPTER 15

Darlene's business was off a bit with so much of the town now out of work, but Ella Mae, Wally, and Phil kept their Saturday, Tuesday, Thursday breakfast routine.

"Pathetic as this sounds," Ella Mae volunteered, "this is the extent of my social life ... having breakfast with you two deadbeats."

"That IS pathetic," Wally agreed. "But Dagwood's always happy to see you."

Darlene came over to the table. "Good morning, beautiful people, would you like the eggs benedict or the orange/cranberry scones?" neither of which Darlene would ever serve or, for that matter, know how to make.

"Go to hell," Ella Mae replied, displaying her trademark, one-lower-front-tooth-missing smile.

"Okay, your regulars," Darlene countered, "and, you know the rules, no damn substitutes."

"That's what I love about this place," Phil offered, "courteous, professional, cheerful service."

Darlene was already on her way to the kitchen, so either didn't hear Phil or chose to ignore one of her most favorite regulars.

Ella Mae lowered her voice and leaned closer to Wally and Phil. "Either of you hear anything worth sharing?"

"Well, both our fearless police chief and the top homicide guy from the state have been making the rounds," Wally responded.

"They talk with you?" Ella Mae asked.

"Naw, why'd they want to talk with me? I'm just a tiny tadpole in a big pond."

"How about you, Phil."

"No. They talk with you, Ella Mae?"

"No. But if they do, I think I'll confess just for the hell of it. I'm prepared to throw them off any way I can, so whoever did this continues to fly free as a bird."

Upon hearing the word "bird" Dagwood interrupted with several repetitions of "pretty bird."

"They might accept your confession," Wally said, enjoying the back and forth. "You might want to reconsider."

"Well, as I said awhile back, the food and service up at Moundsville is pretty good and, as screwed up as the system is, they'd never get around to executing me."

Darlene brought their food, then said, "Scoot over Phil. What are you guys hearing?"

"Ella Mae just confessed," Wally said, straight-faced.

Darlene sputtered with laughter, nearly choking.

"You mean that sweet little lady across the table? Well, hell, what are we waiting for? Let's have a parade. We'll rename the park in your honor, Ella Mae.

"No, seriously," Darlene said, "any news to report?"

"Not much," Ella Mae responded, "I hear they've spent time with Beverly, Jake, Miss Florence. They talk with you?"

"Only Frank so far. He knows folks come in here and talk as well as eat and drink, so he wants to hear what I hear. I feel kind of sorry for him. No one wants this thing solved. Unless it was some guy from somewhere else who caught Russell screwing his wife."

"And even if that was the case," Phil said, "I'd feel a bit sorry for the guy."

"Me, too," Wally, who had been concentrating on his breakfast, added.

"I like Frank," Ella Mae said, "but he's not getting any help from me."

"Well, Missy," Darlene said, sliding out of the booth, "you've already confessed, so he doesn't need anything else."

"Case solved," Wally concluded.

CHAPTER 16

Robbie Brownell, sales and marketing manager at Kincaid, was hired by Junior Kincaid, and supervised Russell Kincaid for a short time when he worked in sales. The word was that Robbie was good at what he did and got along with Russell better than almost anyone else in the company.

Frank arranged to meet at Robbie's house, one of the nicest in Waterford. Frank knew who Robbie was but did not know him well.

"Thanks for seeing me," Frank opened.

"Happy to do so. All I've been doing lately is sending out resumes. It's nice to take a break."

"What was your relationship with Russell?" Frank asked. "You two get along?"

"Yeah, we were okay. I know that even before Russell dumped the company a lot of people weren't crazy about him. I loved his dad; miss him to this day. Never knew his grandfather; that was before my time. But, yeah, I got along with Russell."

"Did you know he was thinking about selling the business?"

"I didn't have a clue. When I saw folks I didn't know going in and out of Russell's office, I thought he might be trying to acquire something. Or, maybe hire someone to do the detail part of his job."

"Did you feel at all threatened?"

"No. Russell knew I was pretty good at what I did. I worked hard to market our products and make sure our customers were happy."

"How are you feeling now that Russell sold out, is dead, and you are looking for work?"

"Like everybody else, I'm extremely disappointed about the shutdown. I still cannot believe Russell is dead. And I sure didn't expect to be looking for a job."

"Were you aware Russell was thinking of firing Jake Walter?"

"I knew there was some friction between the two but, no, I hadn't heard that."

"Can you think of anyone — current or past employee — who might be mad enough to kill Russell?"

"I really can't. I mean, what would that accomplish? He'd sold the business. That was a done deal. Killing Russell wasn't going to bring it back."

"Anyone you can think of who's especially hot-tempered?"

"No, not really. But Jake was frustrated, maybe more than the rest of us."

"Frustrated enough to kill Russell?"

"Oh, no. I'd be shocked. Then, again, I'm no psychologist or criminologist."

"Before Russell sold out, did he fire anyone?"

"I don't think so. Jake and I were the only two in the business who reported directly to Russell, and before that, to his dad. So, I think I'd know if he had."

Talking with Robbie, Frank could see why he was in charge of sales and marketing. His friendly, professional manner would relate well with customers.

"Did you think you might be offered a job with Allied? Wouldn't it have made sense to hire you because of your experience and the customer relationships you had?"

"Yes, it would have. But the deal Russell worked out with Allied didn't include any of us. I've heard from a lot of customers and they think the way things were done was shitty and dumb. But, I've got to move on. I need another fifteen or so years somewhere before I can think of retiring."

"One more question," Frank said. "Did Russell explain why you would not be asked to join him at Allied?"

"The only thing he said was that this was the deal Allied wanted."

Frank asked Robbie to contact him if he had any additional thoughts or if he heard anything that might be helpful.

It was Robbie's turn to ask a question. "Do you think you'll be able to solve this?"

"Too early to tell, but the state's involved and it has a lot of resources, so I'm hopeful. We take it personally when a murderer is running around out there." Then Frank repeated what he'd said to others: "We need everyone's help even though most folks believe Russell got what he deserved. No one should want a murder to go unsolved."

CHAPTER 17

Since Allied chose not to employ any Kincaid employees, the personnel files were, for now, still at the plant.

Spence wanted access to those files and, with the help of the Cleveland Police Department, got Allied's permission to enter the practically empty plant and retrieve them. If Allied refused the request, Spence was prepared to seek a court order.

With the assistance of former Human Resources Manager Agnes Carney and Florence Treadwell, two of Spence's men began digging through file drawer after file drawer, looking for names of employees who had been disciplined or terminated.

It turned out there weren't many. People hired seemed to do their jobs satisfactorily, so turnover was minimal. No disciplinary actions or terminations had occurred during Russell's brief tenure as sole owner, and those in the relatively recent years before were mostly entry-level hires warned or let go for attendance issues. Nothing to suggest any lingering hostility. Certainly nothing that would drive a person to commit murder.

There had been only one murder of a local the past ten years and that one had stemmed from a domestic squabble that turned violent. Bar fights were the more common occurrence, but they rarely resulted in more than a broken nose or a few stitches.

+ + +

Another day began with Spence in Frank's office, drinking coffee and reviewing where things stood.

They had been expecting the coroner's report, and Spence had brought it in that morning. Cause of death: 30 caliber bullet wound to head. Time of death: 12-24 hours prior to discovery. Time in water: 12-18 hours.

"We can be damn sure it was a 30 30 deer rifle. Everyone for miles around has one of those," Frank said. "Good old Winchester 30 30, the best ever made. I've got twelve deer with mine over the years, one of them the biggest buck you ever saw. His rack is on the wall in my family room."

"So, what you're saying, Frank, is that among our several hundred or so suspects, most of them have a 30 30."

"I expect that's right."

"And how many might be registered?"

"Maybe three or four."

"Ducky."

Next on the agenda: Russell's car still hadn't turned up, despite the all points bulletin that had been issued describing it. Finding the vehicle might provide answers to where Russell was shot, where he was dumped in the river, and maybe contain physical evidence. Without the car, those questions were unanswered and that physical evidence was unavailable.

"I just hope it's not in Mexico, torn all apart," Spence said.

"If that's the case, maybe we ought to be thinking more about a hit job. That's the kind of stuff mobsters do."

"I'll continue to keep my fingers crossed somebody finds it," Spence said. "That's the kind of break we need."

CHAPTER 18

Spence Atkins had been talking with his counterparts in Homicide at the Cleveland PD. So far, not much of significance had turned up.

Cleveland detectives had talked with Elise Fortney, Russell Kincaid's administrative assistant/lover, and with senior managers at Allied.

Elise repeated what she had told Frank Wharton when he phoned to tell her of Russell's murder. She was sure the killer was someone in Waterford. "Who else would even think of killing him?" she asked. The only name she came up with was Jake Walter, also a repeat of what she had told Frank.

The detectives had asked about threats to Russell, and Elise gave the same answer she'd given before. "Russell got them, but he wouldn't say who he thought they were from."

They said she broke into tears several times during the interview.

When asked about her relationship with Russell, she said they were in love and planned to get married, though no firm date had been set. Meantime, she would work as his administrative assistant at Allied in Cleveland.

Asked if she knew of any women Russell had prior relationships with, Elise became defensive. "I don't know anything about that. I do know that his ex is a very bitter person."

"Bitter enough to have him killed?" they asked. "I don't know. Maybe." Spence made a note to mention this to Frank. Either he or Frank or both needed to pay Beverly another visit.

The detectives told Spence that Allied had beefed up its security in the days since the murder for fear there could be other targets within the company. No threats to anyone else at Allied had been received, but they figured better safe than sorry.

Spence now was leaning more and more toward thinking the murder may have been a well-planned contract hit. At least some of the signs pointed in that direction: one, they had not been able to locate the vehicle; two, Russell was stripped naked when found; three, he was killed by a single, well-placed shot; and, four, he was dumped in a river. This looked more and more like an execution. And, based on having investigated several mob-related murders before, Spence saw similarities.

The Cleveland police told Spence they had some carefully cultivated informants within a couple of badly depleted crime families but, so far, weren't getting any leads. They promised to keep at it, though.

Meantime, in Waterford, Frank Wharton had talked with both Albert Price and Milt Bowman, the two "hotheads" Augie Martino, the bar owner, had mentioned. Both had minor records. Price had two DUIs; Bowman, one spousal abuse. After separate, hour-long meetings, Frank concluded that while they shared the motive of lost jobs, they lacked the smarts to carry out the murder and make Russell's car disappear. Nevertheless, they would remain as "persons of interest."

It was time for another visit with Florence Treadwell, this time to gather more personal information about Russell Kincaid for Spence.

"Miss Florence, we're following up on a lot of stuff," Frank opened. "When you and I talked, we didn't get much into Russell's personal life. You had a unique relationship with the Kincaid family. I know Junior Kincaid and his wife, Elizabeth, before she died, considered you a member of their family."

"And I considered them members of my family," Florence replied. "They were lovely people. I cried and cried when Elizabeth died. Cancer is such an awful disease, and she put up such a courageous fight.

"Junior took her passing very hard. She held that family together. If she had lived longer she might have been able to moderate Russell's behavior. He was a challenge as a teenager ... always getting into things.

"You know that, Frank. You kept him overnight once after he'd pumped gas at the Esso station and sped off without paying."

Frank shook his head. "Yep. He wasn't much into obeying the law.

"Miss Florence, it's well-known Russell was very active sexually. What can you tell me about who he dated, whose sexual favors he may have paid for, and where he went to satisfy his desires?"

Not surprisingly, Florence seemed a bit uneasy getting into this subject. But Frank felt certain Junior Kincaid and she had talked about Russell's escapades.

"I know he slept with a lot of young women. His father was very upset about this but Russell went his own way. As best I could tell, Russell wasn't really serious about any of them.

"I felt so sorry for Beverly. She and Russell had been love birds ever since high school, so we all expected a lasting marriage. But he had to go out and ruin it. Things got to the point where Beverly couldn't stand his cheating any more. It became so well known that it was incredibly embarrassing to her. You know the story from there on. She filed for divorce and things became very contentious and public. It was very embarrassing for Junior, but Russell was beyond his control."

"Miss Florence," Frank resumed, "now that you've had more time to think about who might have killed Russell, do you have anything you believe might be helpful?"

"No, I really don't. You asked me about Jake Walter. Jake would never do such a thing."

"What about Beverly? I know the divorce was a couple or three years ago and she got the house, the BMW, and a bunch of money in the final settlement, but she was still plenty upset."

"I don't blame her for being upset," Florence said. "What Russell did was unforgivable. But if you are asking me if Beverly was somehow involved in Russell's death, the answer is 'no'. She was trying to move on.

"I still think someone not related to Waterford killed him. I believe his promiscuous behavior caught up with him."

"That's certainly a possibility," Frank agreed. "Do you know the identity of any of the women he had relations with?"

"No direct knowledge, but I've heard he had an off and on relationship with a waitress at The Charleston Club downtown."

"Do you know her name?"

"No, I never knew it, and it never came up in the divorce back and forth."

CHAPTER 19

The Charleston Club was founded in the early 1900s by the heads of a couple of prosperous coal and railroad companies. For years, its membership was men only. Only recently had women been allowed to join, and their numbers remained small. It was the place where deals were made, political careers were launched or destroyed, and bad behavior could be concealed. Once an initial membership was established, most of what followed was by legacy.

Legacy is how Russell Kincaid got in. His grandfather was a member, as was his father. Russell enjoyed escaping Waterford for afternoons of dominos, cigars, and conversation at the club. Most of all, he liked booking one of the half-dozen overnight guest rooms where he could have a night of sexual pleasure shielded from prying eyes. Russell became what the club staff considered "a regular."

No one at the club kept score, but Oscar, who had been the doorman for nearly 30 years, was overheard commenting to an associate, "I think the young Kincaid is going for the record" in terms of escorting young women upstairs to a guest room.

Names were never asked or volunteered. The privacy of members was of paramount importance.

✦✦✦

Frank suggested Spence be the one to go to The Charleston Club. Someone from the State Police would have a better chance of getting information than a cop from Waterford.

Spence, dressed in plainclothes, displayed his badge at the front door and was ushered into a small room outside the club manager's office.

After a wait of 15 minutes, a tall, slender, impeccably-dressed gentleman likely in his late sixties emerged and extended his hand.

"Harrison Wainwright, Detective Atkins. Come in. Have a seat. Can I get you anything?"

"No, thanks."

Spence got right to the point. "We are investigating the murder of one of your members ..."

"Yes," Wainwright interrupted, "Mr. Kincaid. A fine young gentleman. What a tragedy."

Spence continued. "We know he came here regularly and we also know he developed a relationship with one of your employees."

"I doubt that, Detective. We have a firm policy ..."

It was Spence's turn to interrupt. "Mr. Wainwright, we know this to be a fact." Spence knew he was stretching the truth in saying this, but he had to grab the stuffy old fart's attention.

"If you don't know who this person is, which I doubt is the case, tell me who does."

Wainwright stiffened. "I believe you have inaccurate ..."

"Mr. Wainwright, we can continue this conversation here or you can come to headquarters and have it with me and several of my associates. Your choice."

"Detective, the privacy of our members ..."

Again, Spence interrupted. "Let me remind you, we are investigating the murder of one of your members. We know Russell Kincaid came here often and we know he had a relationship with one of your servers. Now, you can tell me who that is or, if you prefer, I can interrogate each and every one of them."

Wainwright didn't like being spoken to in such an abrupt, demanding manner. The Charleston police had shown deference toward the club over the years. The attitude had always been, a la Las Vegas, "what goes on in the club, stays in the club." Now, along comes this state cop with all his demands.

"May I make a call?" he asked Spence.

"Be my guest."

Wainwright explained the situation to whomever he called, obviously and uncomfortably seeking permission to break from tradition.

Hanging up, he called out to his secretary, "See if Miss Salisbury is here and, if so, please ask her to come to my office."

A strikingly attractive woman appeared, immaculately dressed in a black skirt, white blouse and white apron.

"Monica, this is Detective Atkins from the State Police. Detective Atkins, this is Monica Salisbury."

The pleasant smile she displayed upon entering, disappeared in an instant.

Shaking hands, Spence turned to Wainwright, "As I am sure you appreciate, I need to talk with Ms. Salisbury in private."

Irritated but knowing he had no choice, Wainwright directed the two into a smaller office next to his.

Closing the door, Spence turned on his best gentle self and began the process of explaining why he needed to talk with Monica. Then came his first question.

"What was your relationship with Mr. Kincaid?"

"He was one of our members."

"I know that, but you and he had a relationship beyond that."

She became noticeably more nervous.

"I don't know what you mean. I work here. I do my job."

Spence zeroed in. "I have it on good authority that you and Mr. Kincaid were lovers."

Monica slumped and held her face in both hands.

Spence waited patiently for her to say something.

Raising up, tears welling in her eyes, she said, "I need this job, Sir. They will fire me."

"No one needs to know what you tell me. That's why it's only the two of us in this room." Spence felt the need to reassure her. "You are not a suspect. But I need you to answer a few questions."

It was clear the words "not a suspect" had the desired, somewhat relaxing effect. Monica took a breath and straightened up.

"When were you and Mr. Kincaid last together?"

Taking another deep breath and looking past Spence, she replied. "Sometime the week after Christmas."

"Where?"

Another pause and then, "Here, upstairs."

Did you hear from him after that?"

"Yes, we talked by phone almost every evening. But he was in the process of moving to Cleveland, so he wasn't able to come to the club."

"Had he said when he might be able to come?"

"Yes, he thought it would be February first."

"Did he come then? Did he call?"

"No." The strain showed in Monica's face. "And then," tears beginning to flow, "I heard ..."

"That he'd been killed," Spence said.

"Yes."

"How would you describe your relationship."

"We were in love. He said he wanted to marry me."

Spence hoped he hadn't shown any reaction to what she said. But, in silence, he wondered how many other women had been told the same thing. What a rotten s.o.b.

"Did Mr. Kincaid ever tell you he feared for his life?"

"No, but sometimes he seemed tense."

"Did he talk about his divorce, his ex-wife?"

"Only that she had divorced him and that he was glad no children were involved."

"When did you and he become involved?"

"Two years ago last October."

"You met here?"

"Yes, I had served him a number of times and he asked me to be one of the servers at a small private party he hosted."

"What about work? Did he talk about his job, about the company?"

The tears had dried and Monica resigned herself to being responsive.

"He said he was hated because he sold the business."

Spence waited to see if Monica would elaborate. She didn't.

"Did he mention the name of anyone who hated him?"

"I'm not sure but I think he mentioned someone who worked directly with him. Is there a Jack?"

"You mean Jake? Jake Walter? Is that the name?"

"Yes. That's it."

"Did he say anything else about Jake Walter?"

"No. Just that they didn't get along."

Spence leaned back before speaking. "Is there anything else you'd like to say?"

"No, sir." And then she broke into tears. "We loved each other. We were going to get married and have a life together. I still can't believe he's gone. Please find out who did this."

Spence did what he'd never done before in a similar situation, he gave Monica a hug while again thinking what a miserable scumbag Kincaid was.

On his way out of the club, Spence told Wainwright how fortunate the club was to have Monica as an employee. He hoped it would help her keep her job.

CHAPTER 20

Spence shared with Frank and Don Blackford, his boss, the detail of his visit to The Charleston Club.

Together, they shook their heads at how Russell strung women along. Spence said he was certain Monica wasn't a suspect. Also, that he thought she had told him everything she knew.

They agreed ex-wife Beverly needed to be considered as a possible. Maybe Elise in Cleveland.

"Jake Walter's name keeps coming up," Spence said. "We need to press him harder. I'll pay him a visit.

"What about Florence Treadwell?" he asked. "She got the double whammy from Russell; demoted and then terminated. Plus, she had a history with the family."

Frank grimaced, "I just don't see her orchestrating it. I may be wrong; it wouldn't be the first time."

Don had been absorbing the back and forth. "So, here's where I think we are. Jake Walter, alone or with help, could have done it. And the ex-wife, the gal in Cleveland, and Miss Treadwell are all possibles for having arranged the hit.

"Agreed," said Spence and Frank in near unison.

"Well, that was easy," Don said with a smile. "Now what?"

Spence took the lead. "I'll visit Jake. I'll fill Cleveland in on my talk with Monica Salisbury in Charleston and ask them to talk further with Elise Fortney at Allied. Those guys in Cleveland know what they're doing, so they may ask Ms. Fortney about Monica. In fact, I'll suggest they do that. It might spark something. Scorned, cheated-on women sometimes open up.

"Frank, I think you need to continue to be the point person with the ex-wife and Florence. Feel free with the ex-wife to mention the Charleston waitress. I leave to you how you go about trying to extract anything more from Florence. She seems a tougher nut to crack."

"That's right," Frank said. "I don't doubt Miss Florence is smart enough to have orchestrated this. I just don't believe she did."

It was a little after two in the afternoon. Frank hadn't eaten anything since breakfast and he hadn't checked in with Darlene lately. After exchanging greetings with the ever-present Dagwood, he took a seat toward the rear, away from the windows that faced the street.

"Hi, Hon. You look a little tuckered. I'll get you some sweet tea while you check out the menu."

Not feeling all that imaginative, Frank decided on a BLT.

Darlene brought it along with a heaping side of potato salad and, without asking, sat across the booth from him.

"So, you issuing a lot of parking tickets these days?" she asked in her charming, smart-ass way.

Frank smiled. "Not all that many. Kinda busy with some other stuff. Are you hearing anything I might want to hear?"

"Oh, silly me," Darlene responded. "I thought you just came in for lunch, not to interrogate me."

"So?" Frank waited.

"Nothing really. Heard there might be some tie-in relating to The Charleston Club."

Frank didn't respond but wondered how in hell she knew that.

"Nobody's come in here confessing?"

"Only Ella Mae. She's looking to go to the Moundsville Bed & Breakfast."

That caused Frank to enjoy his first laugh for longer than he could remember. He knew Ella Mae; she'd say anything and everything — the more preposterous the better.

Frank purposely did not get on Darlene's case for talking to Miss Florence after he'd told her not to. It didn't do any harm, and he didn't want to risk the relationship he had with her. He figured her ability to communicate faster than the speed of light might come in handy if he ever wanted to spread some truth or rumor.

And, where else could he go and have a parrot so happy to see him?

CHAPTER 21

Waterford Mayor Steve Insley had moved quickly in response to the sudden loss of more than 200 jobs. He'd called an emergency meeting of the Town Council that Saturday. Then he'd followed up with Congressman Jay Bosworth to see if the closure had violated any laws. It hadn't.

His next move was to contact the West Virginia Economic Development Department to see if it was working with any companies that might be interested in setting up shop in Waterford. Insley was told to contact Allied to determine if it planned to sell or lease the property. With that information, Economic Development could list and promote it.

Insley was the second-generation owner of Valley Hardware. He, like his father before him, loved the hardware business, and it had grown over the years, thanks in no small part to Kincaid Fabricators' prosperity. Kincaid was the economic anchor. And, because its business was steady, not cyclical, Waterford and businesses like Insley's didn't experience the sharp ups and downs many other communities did.

Bottom line, Insley was going to do everything he could to rescue his home town and, in the process, protect his own business.

Realizing tensions between the people of Waterford and Allied Manufacturing ran high, he nevertheless initiated a call to the Cleveland company.

Alfred Donaldson was Allied's president and the person with whom Russell Kincaid had struck the deal to sell Kincaid and terminate its workforce. Insley left two messages before hearing back.

He made clear in his message he simply was interested in learning Allied's plans for the physical structure it had left behind. Were they going to try to sell or lease it?

It took a couple of days, but Donaldson returned the calls. He told Insley they hadn't made any firm decisions but he thought selling would be the way to go.

"Do you have a price in mind?" Insley asked.

"No, not yet. Why? Do you have a potential buyer?"

Insley said he didn't, and then told Donaldson about his conversation with the Economic Development office. He explained his interest was the local economy.

Insley kept the conversation cordial. He wasn't about to reveal the hostility he felt. Better to be civil in case some way could be found to acquire the structure and attract some business to come to town and hire at least a bunch of what had been Kincaid employees.

He and Donaldson exchanged cell phone numbers and agreed to keep the lines of communication open.

Two days later, while in his store, Insley recognized an incoming call was from Donaldson.

"Mr. Donaldson?"

"Call me Al, please."

"Okay. And I am Steve." Oh, after decimating my town, we're now on a first-name basis, he thought.

"Steve, I appreciated your call the other day. I know there's a lot of anger and disappointment in your town, but what we did was the right thing for our company. That's what it boiled down to. I suppose we might have handled the communications better, but what's done is done."

Insley let Donaldson continue without interrupting.

"I talked things over with our board of directors, and we decided we'd like to explore selling the plant. We're going to have it appraised and I'll get back to you with what we come up with. It's a good, solid building."

"Yes it is," Insley agreed. "The Kincaids upgraded it steadily over the years and it was well maintained.

"When do you think you might get back to me with a price?"

"I hope within a couple of weeks. Then I would appreciate your help in talking with the state."

"I'll be happy to help."

Hanging up, Insley felt good about the conversation and the door he'd opened. Nothing good may come of it but, as his father used to say, "Nothing beats failure but a try." He guessed he could have unloaded on Donaldson about the damage done to Waterford, but that wouldn't have accomplished anything. At least — and for now — he had a working relationship with Donaldson. He'd see what, if anything good, that produced.

CHAPTER 22

Several weeks passed and still no car and no indication where Russell had been dumped into the Maplethorn. Spence and Frank agreed the likelihood was that he'd been tossed over the Haggin Bridge, five miles upriver of town. No evidence had been found on the bridge but they figured the river's flow could well have carried the body down to Wilkens Ferry Landing in the time period they were dealing with.

The bullet had been extracted from Russell's skull, but no shell casing found, so tying it to a specific 30 30 rifle was impossible.

No one, other than Ella Mae, had stepped forward to admit guilt. Spence wondered if Ella Mae might have had something to do with the murder, but Frank discounted that possibility. Ella Mae was always saying crazy things. That was Ella Mae.

The Cleveland police had asked, in the course of their follow up with Elise Fortney, if she was aware of Russell's ongoing affair with "an unnamed woman in Charleston."

They said she stiffened and her face flushed. No tears this time. Then she replied that people were just trying to destroy Russell's name at a time when he could no longer defend himself. She did not specifically say the report was untrue, and one of the officers included in his notes that her response was half-hearted. He wrote, "I believe the information we provided confirmed something she didn't want to hear but feared was true."

Spence opted not to phone in advance. Frank had provided directions, so Spence appeared at Jake Walter's house unannounced.

As had been the case when Frank had interviewed him, Jake was in the garage, continuing to work on his restoration project.

After introducing himself and showing his badge, Spence followed Jake into the house. Jake introduced Spence to his wife and then suggested he and Spence talk in the den.

Jake appeared a little surprised by Spence's visit, figuring if any more questions needed to be asked they'd come from Frank. He also appeared a bit uneasy in the presence of a State of West Virginia homicide cop.

"I know you've talked with Chief Wharton," Spence began. "We are working closely together on this case. As you may know, the state's in charge of homicides, but Frank is a great help."

Jake shifted a bit in his chair while staring intently at Spence.

"We're talking to a bunch of people," Spence continued, "and you worked directly with Russell Kincaid."

"Yes, that's right," Jake replied, dreading the kinds of questions he expected would follow.

"You two didn't get along, isn't that right?"

"I wouldn't put it that way," Jake said. "I did my job."

"But you had some disagreements."

"Yes, that's fair to say."

"Like what?"

"Oh, things like production schedules, preventive maintenance, things like that."

"Do you think he felt threatened by you?"

"No. Hell, he owned the company. He could do as he pleased."

"Was your job in jeopardy?"

"Frank asked me that question. No."

"We've picked that up from others ..."

Jake interrupted, exhibiting for the first time a bit of irritation, "I don't know anything about that. I had a job to do. I knew what I was doing."

"Are you saying Russell didn't?"

"No. But ask anybody. Who knew more about the business, Russell or me? Who knew every employee by name, Russell or me? Who knew our customers, Russell or me?"

Jake realized he was getting more than a little bit defensive but the hell with it. Russell Kincaid was a friggin' joke, a shell of what his father had been. And that friggin' joke had cost Jake and more than 200 others pain beyond belief.

"Were you upset when Russell demoted Florence Treadwell?" Spence asked.

That really rung a bell.

"I was mad as hell. What he did was downright cruel. Miss Florence is respected by everyone. No one worked harder than she did. No one was more dedicated to the business or knew more about it. She was a God damn treasure, and he tossed her aside like a piece of crap and brought in that little bitch to replace her."

Jake realized the moment he said "that little bitch" he'd made a mistake, lost his cool. "I'm sorry. I shouldn't have said that. But, damn it, what he did to Miss Florence is unforgivable."

The more Spence was hearing, in content and tone, the more he was thinking Jake may well have been mad enough to kill Russell.

Spence figured he had Jake churned up enough that the time was right to ask him if he had anything to do with the murder.

"I can fully understand your anger," he started. "After having worked for someone you respected, you now were stuck working for someone you didn't. Then, that person discarded a person you and everyone else respected. And, finally, he sold the business and terminated everyone, you included. I don't blame you for being mad as hell. Didn't you feel a strong urge to get even, to make that miserable creature pay a price?"

"Yeah, I was mad. We all felt betrayed."

"Mad enough to do something about it?"

"If you're asking did I kill Russell, the answer is no."

"Mad enough to somehow be involved in his death?"

"No, damn it, no!" The volume of Jake's voice climbed several decibels.

Spence paused to make a few notes. That allowed Jake a few seconds to wonder how much longer the interrogation was going to last and to believe Spence may have made up his mind Jake pulled the trigger.

"Okay," Spence resumed, "if not you, if you were not involved, who? I'm sure you must have given this some thought."

"Yeah. But I don't know. You're the detective, I'm not."

"You don't know, but who or what are the possibilities?"

Jake heaved a sigh. Maybe it was time to try to shift the blame, to steer Spence and Frank in another direction. "I suppose Beverly Kincaid might have arranged it. She hated Russell. I've even thought it could have been part of Allied's plan: grab our company and then dispose of Russell."

"Why might Allied do that?"

"Because it got what it wanted: our business. To get that, it had to take Russell as part of the deal. And Russell was a negative, not a positive. He didn't add any value. He'd be a pain in the butt, an expense they didn't want."

"But to feel the need to kill him? Is that what you're suggesting?" Spence asked.

"It's a possibility. You asked me for possibilities. I don't know those people at Allied but I'm clear on one point. They didn't give a damn about all the lives they were devastating here in Waterford. So, who the hell knows what they might be capable of?"

Spence didn't react but thought to himself. Jesus! That sounds a little crazy but it just might make sense. Allied would get Russell Kincaid out of its hair and make sure his body surfaced in Waterford where local suspects would number in the hundreds. He'd discuss this theory with Cleveland Homicide. He needed to know more about Allied and how it did business.

Jake sensed Spence absorbed what he had said and, inwardly, was proud of himself for suggesting the possibility.

"Any other theories," Spence asked.

"No." Jake was tempted to elaborate but decided not to.

After leafing through several pages of his notes, Spence asked, "You mentioned Beverly Kincaid as a possibility. What more can you tell me?"

"I didn't know Beverly all that well, but she was one furious women at the time they went through their divorce."

"But that was a couple of years ago. Was she upset with the settlement she got?"

"I don't think it was that. I heard she got a lot of money and the house, which is a really nice one. I think it was the public embarrassment he put her through. He didn't pull any punches; but then, neither did she. You heard about her bumper sticker, didn't you?"

"Yeah. That's a classic," Spence responded.

"She used to always be out and about in town. She was involved as a volunteer in a lot of stuff. But since the divorce, you rarely see her. I've heard she's got friends in Charleston and Parkersburg but she doesn't spend time with folks here any more."

"But you think she might have had something to do with ..."

Jake interrupted. "Hey, I don't know. I just know she was raging mad when they were going through the divorce."

"One final question: On the assumption that no one at the company felt more mistreated, more betrayed than Florence Treadwell, do you believe she could have had something to do with Russell's murder?"

"No way. Absolutely not. Never in a million years."

Driving back to Frank's office, Spence consolidated his thinking into three pieces. One, Jake remained a prime suspect. Two, Jake raised a plausible theory involving Allied Manufacturing. And, three, though it was unlikely Miss Florence had anything to do with the murder, the possibility she did was still alive.

CHAPTER 23

Spence shared with Frank the content of his talk with Jake. Frank hadn't thought about Allied's possible interest in getting rid of Russell either.

"As soon as we finish, I'll get Cleveland busy doing some research on Allied. Things like other deals they've done, their reputation, background on the guys who run it. I wonder if anyone there has a record?"

Jake had made a point that registered. Allied was incredibly ruthless in the way it acquired Kincaid and terminated its employees. Who knows what else they might have done? Murder someone they no longer needed?

Meantime, Frank had followed up again with both Beverly Kincaid and Florence Treadwell.

Beverly seemed a little irritated Frank felt the need to talk with her again.

"Frank, I've told you everything I know. I may have spoken to Russell once or twice since our divorce. One time I remember asking him who he'd used to replace the house hot water heater. I can't remember what we talked about the other time. I do know they were very short conversations and neither was within the last year. So, I don't know what else you hope I might be able to say."

Frank wanted to see how she might react to what Spence had learned from Monica Salisbury at The

Charleston Club. He didn't reveal Monica's name but said, "A young lady in Charleston has told us she was having an ongoing affair with Russell that began two or three years ago and that Russell had said he wanted to marry her."

"I don't doubt it for a minute," Beverly replied, closing her eyes and tilting her head back.

"Did you know about this one?" Frank asked.

"I'm not sure. But she was one of many. Our marriage had become a joke, a vicious, ugly joke. I'm sorry he's dead. But he put me through absolute hell. I tried for awhile to keep us together, to forgive and forget. At first, he denied everything. Then, he promised to stop. But he lied time after time. He played me for a fool. Finally, I'd had all I could take. At least now, he can't hurt anyone else."

Believing he already knew the answer, Frank asked, "Beverly, are you the beneficiary on any insurance policies Russell may have had? Is there any way you benefited financially from his death?"

"No and no," she responded, again showing slight irritation. "I wish that was the case, but everything I'm going to get I already got in the settlement. I promise you that. Check it out. Maybe he provided for 'Miss Charleston' and others."

Frank had gone into this follow-up interview with low expectations and nothing Beverly said provided anything new.

"I wish I could help you, Frank, because the people of this town deserve an answer. I intend to continue living here. It's my home. I just wish this could be solved quickly so everyone can get on with their lives."

"I know I asked you this previously," Frank said, "but can you think of anyone who might have done this?"

"Not one, maybe 200 or so," she responded, shaking her head.

Frank was done with his questioning. Beverly had accurately described the dilemma he, Spence, and Don Blackford faced. It wasn't quite like looking for a needle in a haystack ... but pretty damn close.

The follow-up with Miss Florence didn't produce anything either. He shared details of the Charleston Club story with her as well in the hope it might stimulate some additional nugget of information.

Miss Florence's only reaction was, "I'll never understand how he could be so unlike his father. Everything his father was, Russell was the opposite. I guess that's not unique in families, but it's a puzzlement to me.

"I feel so sorry for Beverly. She went through so much with that man. Now it's all being dredged back up again. I'm surprised she doesn't move somewhere. I would."

Frank opted not to mention the possibility that Allied might have wanted Russell out of the picture. He could think of no reason to believe she knew anything about Russell's dealings with the people in Cleveland. By then, she had been demoted to accounts payable.

CHAPTER 24

Mayor Steve Insley had not told anyone in Waterford — not even the Town Council members — of his conversation with Alfred Donaldson, the president of Allied Manufacturing. He wanted to hear back from Donaldson on the asking price for the Kincaid building first.

The call from Donaldson came, as Donaldson said he expected it would, about two weeks after their initial conversation.

"Steve," Donaldson began, "the appraisers came back with a figure on the building."

"And ..." Steve waited.

"Everything, including the office furniture we left ... two million."

Insley wasn't in the business of negotiating deals, certainly not of that magnitude. He was the owner of a successful but small hardware store. He thought for a few seconds, then said, "Well, that's a starting point."

"You said you could put me in touch with the state Economic Development folks in Charleston," Donaldson said.

"Yes, I can. I'll make a call and ask them to get back to you directly."

"Sounds good. Do you think your town of Waterford might be interested in making some kind of deal?"

"I wish we could," Insley responded, "but we're in a hell of a fix right now."

Donaldson understood what Insley was saying because Allied's shutting down of Kincaid Fabricators and terminating all of its employees was the sole cause of Waterford's plight.

Immediately after ending the call with Donaldson, Insley phoned his contacts at the Economic Development Department. He walked them through his conversations with Donaldson. Then he asked if they had any prospects that might be interested in the building.

Nothing at this five minutes was the response but, after talking with Donaldson and getting more details, they promised to get busy promoting it.

The call ended after the EDD officials promised to keep Insley informed.

Having covered these bases, Insley used a closed executive session portion of the next Town Council meeting to inform his colleagues of what he had been up to. He expected one or two of the four members would be unhappy he had the conversations with Donaldson without their permission or knowledge. But, perhaps still shell-shocked by what had happened to their town, they weren't. In fact, one of the members who regularly drew joy from second-guessing Insley, thanked him for taking the initiative.

"Two million! That seems like a lot," one commented.

"I agree," Insley responded. "That's the asking price. I'll bet it can be had for less, and I'm sure the EDD folks will suggest something lower to Allied."

The Council members asked about the tone of Insley's conversations with Donaldson.

"We kept things cordial. There's nothing to gain by rubbing their nose in how they screwed our town. They know that. We need to move forward. We need to get someone in that building, someone who will employ our people."

Believing the people of Waterford needed a bit of a lift, Insley and the Town Council scheduled a Town Hall meeting in the Middle School gymnasium. Chairs had been brought in to supplement the bleacher seating, and still some folks had to stand wherever they could find a few feet of space.

Insley opened the meeting with a briefing on where things stood. He told of Allied's intentions to sell and said he had put them in touch with the EDD in Charleston, which would assist in the marketing of the building. He didn't volunteer the asking price, confident that would come up in the questioning. Then he opened the meeting up for questions.

Predictably, the first question was "how much?"

"It'll probably be less than two million," Insley responded, knowing the EDD would be recommending something below what Donaldson had stated.

"Those bastards should give us the damn building after the way they screwed us," a man standing in the back hollered. That produced cheering, fist-pumping, and a smattering of welcome laughter.

Insley then explained that there are some funds the state can try to get from the feds to help subsidize the plant's purchase. "If we can get some of that money, it would make the building more attractive to a potential buyer."

Anger was still alive in the building, but now folks also began to believe there might be a path forward — a path that, in time, might restore all or at least a part of Waterford's economic base.

The Q and A continued for an hour or so until a woman seated in the bleachers took her turn. "Steve." she said, referring to Insley, "speaking for myself and, I believe, for most people here tonight, thank you for being the mayor we need." Applause followed and, with that, the Town Hall was adjourned.

CHAPTER 25

Homicide Detective Spence Atkins drove north to Cleveland to talk with his counterparts in that police department. Prior to this, they'd been in almost daily telephone and email communication. His purpose was to ask them to initiate an investigation into Allied Manufacturing.

He shared the theory that Allied did not want Russell Kincaid in their organization. They had gotten what they wanted — Kincaid Fabricators. Now that they had it, they no longer needed or wanted Russell. To get rid of him would be expensive. He'd demand substantial compensation. Having him "disappear" and be found dead in Waterford, where there would be hundreds of suspects, would be cheaper.

Spence said, "I believe we need to consider this as a possibility. I need you guys to find out everything you can about Allied and the people who run it. I know the company has existed for some twenty years but it's been in the fire hose valve business for only about five. They acquired Kincaid mostly for its patented products.

"Maybe there's something or someone in Allied we need to know more about," Spence continued. "Hell, for all we know, something similar may have happened in the past; maybe someone in the company has violated a law or two."

Cleveland Homicide agreed to expand the scope of its investigation and keep Spence informed. They also agreed that if they needed help, they'd seek it from the local office of the FBI.

Spence left wondering if this theory might prove to be a game changer. Up to now, all of his attention and that of Waterford Police Chief Frank Wharton had been aimed at either terminated Kincaid employees or Russell Kincaid's ex-wife or maybe a lover or two.

"Damn," he said aloud as he drove onto the freeway heading south to Charleston, "this just might be the answer."

Spence hadn't phoned Frank Wharton that evening, deciding the update on his Cleveland meeting could await their regular morning meeting the next day.

Molly, Frank's dispatcher and all-purpose "Girl Friday," had brought in home-baked cinnamon rolls to accompany Spence's and Frank's morning coffee.

"Good Lord, Molly," Spence said, "this case is going to move me up into the heavyweight class if I'm not careful."

"Yeah," Frank said, grabbing at his belt buckle, "I weighed 175 before Molly started working here. "Now I'm 200 and counting."

"You're welcome," Molly said with a giggle as she closed the door so they could talk.

"You know," Spence began, "I'm still thinking Jake Walter is our prime suspect, but the possibility Allied arranged the killing is intriguing. The guys in Cleveland are going to find out everything they can about Allied and the people who run it. And, if they get to the point where they need to, they'll get the FBI involved.

"What are you thinking?" Spence asked.

"I agree the Allied thing is worth exploring. I don't know much about the corporate world except that, like in everything else, there are good and bad people. People who abide by the law and people who break it. I'll be interested to hear what Cleveland comes up with."

Frank then briefed Spence on his meeting with Beverly Kincaid, Russell's ex. "She's about had it with me," he said. "She's not grieving the loss of Russell but she keeps saying she has no idea who might have killed him. I'm in the process of finding out for sure if she had anything to gain from his death. She said she didn't. I expect that's right, that she got everything she was going to get in the divorce settlement. But I'm double-checking to see if she remained as the beneficiary on anything in his estate."

At Spence Atkins' request, the Cleveland Police Department's Homicide Division began its investigation into Allied Manufacturing. The company had shareholders and its stock was publicly traded, so a starting point was to check out its various filings with governmental regulators like the Securities and Exchange Commission. Homicide sought the expertise of its Fraud Division since corporate financial shenanigans was their expertise.

A cursory examination of Allied's filings showed nothing extraordinary. It was heavily leveraged, having borrowed to acquire Kincaid Fabricators and other businesses. But so, too, were many other companies.

Revealing was information showing it borrowed $100 million in late 2016 in connection with acquiring Kincaid. Unstated was whether that was all or a portion of the cost of that transaction.

The detective assigned to head up this part of the Allied investigation was 24-year department veteran, Lieutenant Roscoe Barnes. Armed with information gathered from the company's regulatory filings and with information from Spence Atkins in West Virginia, Barnes made an appointment to meet with Allied's president, Alfred Donaldson.

The shear size of Barnes was intimidating. A college basketball center years before, he stood six feet nine and, because he no longer trained vigorously, his weight had grown to a few pounds short of 300.

In setting the appointment, Barnes hadn't been specific about the subject, only that it related to an investigation. And, he hadn't given Donaldson much time to think about it. He phoned at nine and Donaldson, somewhat reluctantly, agreed to meet him at eleven.

Donaldson figured the meeting was related to the murder of Russell Kincaid, but wasn't certain.

Detective Barnes arrived five minutes early and was ushered into an empty, expensively decorated conference room. A couple of minutes later, Donaldson and a second person he introduced as the corporate legal counsel, John Pendergast, entered. Barnes was used to talking with people accompanied by legal counsel.

"How can we be of help, Detective Barnes?" Donaldson asked.

Barnes said he was part of a team in Cleveland and West Virginia investigating the murder of Russell Kincaid.

"What a tragedy," Donaldson said. "Russell and I put that deal together and he was going to be a key person here at Allied. A tragedy," he repeated.

"I want to ask about his role here at your company," Barnes began. "What was his position?"

Looking at Counselor Pendergast as he answered, Donaldson said, "He was Senior Consultant."

"So, does that mean he was a corporate officer?"

"Not technically, but he certainly was a key adviser."

"Was he happy with that position? It seems to me because he owned the company you acquired, he'd be more than a consultant once the transaction was done. Maybe a senior vice president or executive vice president ... something like that."

"Yes, I'm sure he was happy. We're not all that title conscious around here. We — all of us — were enthusiastic about having completed the acquisition."

"How much did you pay for Kincaid Fabricators? And, was it all cash or a combination of cash and stock?"

Pendergast spoke up at this point. "The parties to the transaction agreed not to disclose the details ..."

Barnes didn't let Pendergast finish. "I won't press you on that today, but I may well need to know the details going forward and, as I expect you know, I will be entitled to get them."

After making a note or two, Barnes looked up and asked, "As senior consultant, what were you paying Mr. Kincaid?"

"Again," Pendergast began, "that is not something we disclose."

"Well, maybe the regulatory agencies don't require it, but I may. And, if I do, I trust you will provide it.

"Now, Mr. Donaldson, and I would appreciate you answering this one. Were you aware of any threats Mr. Kincaid may have received?"

"Yes. He told me he had received some."

"Did he or you take them seriously?"

"He said he wasn't worried."

"Were you?"

"We stepped up security here."

"Before or after Mr. Kincaid was murdered."

"Both. We intensified the effort after his death. Given what had happened, I was concerned for the safety of our people and the security of our facilities. We were in a state of shock. Who in the world would do such a thing?"

"It happens," Barnes said matter of factly.

"Mr. Donaldson, are you fully aware of the impact you have had on the town of Waterford?"

"Yes. But we've been very generous with the severance packages we provided."

"But those are for a short term. More than 200 people who had good-paying jobs now don't."

"Detective Barnes, if it had made good business sense to keep that plant open and those people employed, we would have done so. But it didn't. The deal worked only if we acquired the equipment and ownership of the patents and consolidated everything here."

Barnes didn't say anything but he thought: That's right, business is business; to hell with the people and their town.

Looking at Donaldson and then Pendergast, Barnes asked, "Did either of you or anyone else here receive any threats?"

"No," both replied.

"Do you have any idea who might have murdered Mr. Kincaid?"

"No," Donaldson replied. "I wish we did. And, be assured, Detective, if we did, you would have heard from us."

"Over the years ... not related to this case ... have you ever been physically threatened?"

Both Donaldson and Pendergast said they hadn't.

Donaldson shifted in his chair, leaning back. "Let me go back to your earlier question. I certainly don't know and I shouldn't play detective, but I would think the killer is someone who worked at Kincaid, someone who had it in for Russell."

"Can you give me a name?"

"I'm in no way accusing, okay? But Russell told me he planned to let the plant manager go whether or not we did the deal. He said that guy was trying to undercut him."

"Who was that? Do you have a name?"

Donaldson looked at Pendergast, who answered, "Jacob Walter."

"You know anything else about this Walter person?"

"Just that he'd been there a number of years and, Russell said, was resistant to change."

"Did Walter know about the negotiations you were having with Mr. Kincaid?"

"I'm quite sure he didn't," Donaldson replied. "They were confidential between Russell and us."

Shuffling back through a few pages of his note pad, Barnes returned to an earlier point. "Did Mr. Kincaid have an employment contract with Allied? And, before either of you answer, was it short term or for a number of years?"

Pendergast replied. "Again, Detective, we do not disclose such things."

Barnes couldn't resist. "Mr. Pendergast. You may want to reconsider that decision. This is a homicide investigation. As I said earlier, we can require that information be provided or you can comply voluntarily. Your choice.

Barnes pushed back his chair and straightened up to his full, imposing height. "Gentlemen, that's all for now. I appreciate your meeting with me on short notice. My office or I, personally, will be in touch. Please call me if you have any information you believe I should know. Here's my card. I'm available 24/7."

On the drive back to headquarters, Barnes let his thoughts run freely. He didn't much like either Donaldson or Pendergast. He wasn't prepared to say they had some kind of role in Kincaid's fate, but neither was he prepared to say they didn't. He was confident of one thing, though, talking to the two had not been a waste of time.

CHAPTER 26

Ella Mae was fifteen minutes late for breakfast with Wally and Phil.

"Where you been?" Wally asked, already munching on a biscuit. "We were about ready to send out a search party."

"You think all I have to do is sit here and listen to you two characters?" Ella Mae responded in her usual tough-love manner. "I do have another life."

"Yeah," Phil offered, "and everybody in town's talking about it."

"Go to hell, Philly. You're just jealous," she said, smiling and raising her eyebrows.

"Miss Florence phoned and I lost track of the time."

"Did she confess to shooting Russell?" Wally asked sarcastically.

"No, she said you did it, and Frank is coming after you."

"No, seriously," Wally continued, "did you two talk about our favorite son, Russell?"

Ella Mae leaned across the table and lowered her raspy voice. "They're looking into things in Cleveland. They think there may be some connection. Maybe Allied wanted Russell out of the picture. If that was the case, have someone snuff him out and drop him in the

Maplethorn where we'd find him. Presto: now all of us are suspects."

"Shit, I hadn't thought of that," Phil said. "The friggin' plot thickens."

"You think they'd do something like that?" Wally asked.

"Are you kidding?" Ella Mae responded. "Look what they did to us. They don't give a damn about anything but themselves. I wouldn't put it past them. I think it would be funny as hell if it turns out they had the little shit killed. Justice, sweet justice."

"What else did Miss Florence have to say?" Phil asked.

"She said Frank and the detective from the state are leaning pretty hard on Jake. Jake's getting a little uptight, thinking they believe he might have done it."

Wally, pausing between bits of his ham and eggs, asked, "What do you think?"

"I know he was plenty mad, but I find it hard to believe he'd kill anyone."

"Same here, and I know him really well," Wally responded. "We've hunted and fished together here and in Ohio a couple of days at a time. You get to know someone pretty well when you spend that kind of time together."

"You think he might have got someone else to do it?" Phil asked.

"I guess it's possible. Anything's possible. I'm beginning to wonder if they'll ever solve this thing," Wally said.

"Maybe they'll end up accepting your confession, Ella Mae."

"I wish they would, Wally. I'm tired of my cooking. I'm tired of Darlene's cooking. I'm tired of yakking with you two jerks. And, I'm tired of paying rent. Moundsville is sounding better and better. Think of it, free food, free lodging, and an opportunity to make new friends. Hell, what's not to like?"

"We'd come visit you," Wally offered, "just to piss you off."

"I'd make sure you weren't on my visitors list."

"Okay, are we done?" Phil asked, picking up his check. "See you Thursday. Please try to be on time, Ella Mae."

"Screw you, Philly Boy," Ella Mae said as she blew a kiss his way.

They exchanged goodbyes with Dagwood on their way out.

CHAPTER 27

Detective Barnes of the Cleveland PD reached Spence Atkins and Frank Wharton during their morning meeting in Frank's office in Waterford.

"I don't know where all of this will lead," Barnes said, "but I came away from my meeting with 'your friend', Mr. Donaldson, and his asshole attorney thinking they just may know something about Mr. Kincaid's murder.

"They wouldn't tell me what they paid Kincaid for his company, or what they were paying him to be senior consultant. I didn't expect they would, but we can get the answers to both of those questions.

"It's clear to me they borrowed heavily to acquire Kincaid's equipment and patents. I got copies of Allied's recent press releases and one of them shows they took on one hundred million bucks of new debt in 2016. I don't yet know how much of that was used for the Kincaid acquisition, but I'm guessing most of it was."

"That's some serious money," Spence volunteered.

"Yeah," Frank said. "For our little hometown company."

Barnes continued, "As I said, I don't know what they were paying Kincaid as a consultant. Some of his comp might have been in Allied stock and some in cash. It's possible when I press them some more, they'll provide it. If they don't, we can go to court and get it.

"Also, Allied didn't make Russell Kincaid an officer when they brought him on board. That's a bit unusual, and it may be significant. The SEC requires publicly-traded companies to disclose every year the compensation of its five highest-paid officers. Since Russell wasn't an officer, they weren't required to say what they were paying him. There may not be anything wrong with any of this. I can't say there is. I can't say there isn't. I can say this, however, I came away not liking either Donaldson or his pompous lawyer pal.

"Oh, one other thing, I asked them about threats. They said they hadn't received any but that Kincaid told them he had. Then, a bit later, Donaldson volunteered an opinion. Up to then, he hadn't volunteered anything and had been very restrained in answering my questions. He said, and I think I have his words pretty much verbatim, 'I would think the killer is someone who worked at Kincaid, someone who had it in for Russell'.

"I asked him if he had a name, and, after he looked over at Pendergast, the lawyer, he said, Jacob Walter. Does that name ring any bells with either of you?"

Frank responded, "Yep, Jake Walter was the plant manager."

Barnes continued, "Donaldson said Kincaid told him Jacob Walter had been with the company for a number of years and was resistant to change. I asked if Walter knew about Russell's plan to sell the company, and he said he didn't think so.

"That's all I got, guys. Anything new from your end?"

Spence responded, "Good stuff, Detective. Thanks. We haven't Mirandized anyone. So far, just interviews; no lawyers involved. Jake Walter is the closest thing we have to a prime suspect. There was bad blood between Russell and Jake. We know that for sure."

"Being the local guy," Frank interrupted, "I can add a bit to that. Jake was liked and respected throughout the company. Russell wasn't. Jake was dedicated to the company. Russell wasn't. Jake was really pissed that Russell demoted a beloved person in the company, Florence Treadwell, as soon as he took control.

"I've talked at length with Jake, and so has Spence, and it's clear to both of us that he, like most everyone else in town, was furious at Russell for shutting down the business and terminating everyone. But, no surprise, he denies having anything to do with Russell's death.

"We've also spent a lot of time with Russell's ex-wife. They went through a super nasty divorce a couple or three years ago. He had a well-earned reputation for screwing anyone willing to take their clothes off.

"Since I last met with her, I've been able to confirm she did not benefit financially from his death. She got what she was going to get at the time of the divorce. That diminishes the likelihood that she, somehow, was involved in his murder. But, we haven't eliminated her as a possibility."

"I agree with what Frank said about both Jake Walter and Russell's ex," Spence said. "It's clear neither one of them had any like for Russell. Not one kind word, not one tear shed by either of them."

"You mentioned a Florence Treadwell," Barnes said. "Who's she?"

"Let me answer this one," Frank said to Spence. "She was executive assistant to Russell's father; had been for a long time. Everybody at the plant and in town knows her as "Miss Florence." A classy, very smart woman. Knew everything about the company and, before Russell shoved her aside, was considered a member of the Kincaid family. And, I mean just that, a member of the family.

"The way Russell abruptly demoted her caused a lot of concern in the company and that bled over to the community, where she continues to be loved for her volunteering."

"So, do you think she might be involved?" Barnes asked.

"I can't say for sure, but I don't think so," Frank responded. "Still, we have to consider the possibility that she orchestrated it. She's one of the smartest people I know.

"Detective, did you pick up any indication that Donaldson didn't want Russell hanging around Allied?" Frank asked.

"Nothing direct. But just having him as a consultant rather than an officer might suggest that."

"One other thing," Frank said to Barnes, "Your guys already talked with Elise Fortney, Russell's lover and secretary."

"Yes. I'm aware of that."

"Then you know she was the person Russell promoted to replace Florence Treadwell and was the only Kincaid employee he took with him to Allied."

"Yes. I'll plan to talk with her myself and compare what she tells me to what she said earlier. I'll also see if she continues to be employed by Allied."

"She also pointed the finger at Jake Walter," Frank said. "But I don't attach any special importance to that. I do, though, wonder if she is telling us everything she knows about threats she says Russell received."

Barnes concluded the conversation by saying he'd work at getting answers to the questions concerning what Allied paid to buy Kincaid and what they were paying Russell as a consultant. Also, he'd dig into the backgrounds of Donaldson and the other officers of Allied, and he'd visit with Elise Fortney.

"I'll be back at you."

CHAPTER 28

"What next?" Frank asked Spence after their briefing by Barnes.

"Has Jake Walter ever been in trouble with the law?" Spence asked.

"No," Frank responded. "In fact, with the exception of a couple of regulars at Roadside Bar, no one we've been talking with here in Waterford has so much as a speeding ticket.

"Russell's the one who was always getting into trouble. Nothing all that serious, but he was a handful for his parents. And, whenever I had to deal with him, he always left me with the impression that laws were meant for other folks, not him. He was nothing, and I mean nothing, like his father. His father was a great guy. His mother, too. She died of cancer some years ago. Russell was a know-it-all smart ass."

"Maybe it's time to switch roles," Spence said. "Why don't I go see Florence Treadwell. I expect she won't expand on what she's told you, but I'd like to get a first-hand impression of her."

"Sounds good," Frank said. "At some point, we'll probably want to gain access to Jake Walter's phone records. But I don't think we want to do that until we've covered a few more bases. Also, I want to talk to Elise

Fortney again. But I'll wait until after Barnes has had his conversation with her.

"Meantime, I'm going to check in with Darlene at the diner and find out what she's hearing. I know she'd just as soon we didn't solve this crime, but maybe she'll tell me something we don't already know."

Spence phoned Florence Treadwell shortly after noon and asked if they could meet at two in Frank's office. She agreed to the time but asked him to come to her apartment, which he agreed to.

Frank had prepared him. "Miss Florence will be attired as if she is going out to lunch at a country club," he said. "I doubt if she even owns a pair of shorts or slacks. And, you can bet she'll be wearing heels."

She was dressed as advertised when she answered the door.

"Come in Detective. Frank has told me good things about you."

"Thank you, ma'am," Spence responded. "And he has told me good things about you."

After exchanging a few more pleasantries, Spence began with his questions. "How well do you know Jake Walter?"

"Very well. Jake is a dear friend."

"How difficult was the relationship between him and Russell Kincaid?"

"It was difficult. Jake was trying to make it work. But my sense is that Russell was jealous of the relationship

Jake had with everyone at the plant. And, I think Russell felt insecure even though he owned the company."

"Did you feel the relationship had reached the breaking point?"

"No, not until it happened. Not until it was announced the plant was closing and no one would have a job."

"Did the two of them talk after that announcement?"

"I can't say. By then I was out of the loop; I was down in accounts payable."

"Did you and Jake talk about your frustration with Russell before the shutdown."

"Yes, we shared our frustration. I said to give Russell some time. Let him find his footing, and maybe things would get better. Jake thought I was a little too optimistic. Turns out he was right."

"Are you aware of any threats made to Russell?"

"No. But, again, I was out of the loop."

"Think back, if you will, is there anyone you think might have been mad enough to kill Russell Kincaid?"

"As I believe I said to Frank, I've thought a lot about that and, no, I can't think of anyone."

"And that includes Jake Walter?" Spence asked.

"Oh, yes, Jake would never do such a thing."

"What do you know about Allied Manufacturing?"

"They were relatively new to the valve business. They were in industrial pumps. We were strong in valves."

"Did Russell's father ever have any dealings with Allied?"

"Allied contacted him once, asking if he was interested in selling. He told them no. That was the extent of it. We were not competitors or customers or suppliers."

"Did you know Alfred Donaldson?"

"The president of Allied?"

"Yes."

"No. Again, I knew of Allied and I'd heard his name, but that's all."

"Can you visualize any scenario where, once the acquisition of Kincaid was done, Allied might want Russell out of the picture?"

That question appeared to catch Florence a bit off guard. She squinted her eyes and pursed her lips for a couple of seconds before answering. "I hadn't thought of that."

"Do you think it might be possible?"

"Well, yes. Russell wasn't all that interested in the business, certainly not like his father was. And, because of that, he didn't know all that much about it. He didn't know the manufacturing side and he didn't have a relationship with our customers. So, I guess it makes sense to ask what strengths he brought to Allied."

Florence was beginning to understand where Spence was headed with his questions. "Are you thinking Allied may have had something to do with the murder?" she asked.

"We're examining every possibility; that's what we do in Frank's and my line of work," Spence replied. "What do you think?"

Florence paused, "I think you may be on to something, Detective. I just can't imagine anyone here shooting Russell. I can't. We were devastated when he sold out. And, yes, we were mad, plenty mad. You have to understand what he did to our town, to people's lives. He snatched out our heart and stomped on it," her voice rising, "but to think one of us killed him? I can't imagine that. I know, to one degree or another, everyone who worked at the plant. And I know most people in town. No, I don't believe anyone here did it ... I don't."

CHAPTER 29

Frank ignored his growling stomach, waiting until 2:30 to go to Darlene's for a late lunch. Only one other booth was occupied, and the young family there was in the process of finishing their dessert. Five minutes later, upon hearing Dagwood's distinctive "Bye, Darlin'," Frank was the only customer.

"Frankie," Darlene said, offering up her trademark smile. "Where you been?"

"Out and about."

"Roast pork was our lunch special today. Lots of good comments. You want it?"

"Okay. I need some nourishment."

"I'll put the order in and bring you some sweet tea. We need to talk."

Frank chuckled and thought to himself. You'd think she was doing the investigating, not me.

Darlene put the tea in front of Frank and sat down across from him. "You're going to tell me you've solved Russell's murder case, right?"

"No, I'm saving that news for Wednesday's paper."

Darlene laughed her loud, genuine laugh.

Frank didn't allow time for Darlene to ask another question. "What are you hearing?"

"Really, nothing new. No one other than Ella Mae has confessed."

"Oh, come on, you must have heard something more than that," Frank persisted.

"I hear you and your detective friend are leaning pretty hard on Jake. And, I hear you've been spending a lot of time with Miss Florence.

"You want to know what I think?"

"That's why I'm here ... that, and the roast pork."

"I don't think you're looking in the right place."

"Do tell."

"I think it was a hit job. And I think the people at Allied did it to get, pardon my language, that little shit out of their hair. They had what they wanted. They no longer needed him."

Frank hoped his face didn't reveal what he was thinking. Jeez, this woman doesn't miss a thing. She'd make a damn good cop.

"What do you think of that?" Darlene asked, her face glowing with satisfaction about being so smart.

Not wanting to reveal anything, he replied, "Anything's possible."

Remembering it was Jake who surfaced this Allied theory, Frank was certain Darlene and Jake had been talking. No surprise there.

"Have you seen Jake lately?" he asked.

"Yeah, he and the family were here last night for dinner."

"How's he doing?" Frank asked.

"You and your friend have him nervous. He knows he didn't do anything but he's worried you two think he might have."

Frank didn't respond, turning instead to enjoying his meal. "Yeah, this pork is really good."

"Nothing but the finest gourmet dining right here in beautiful downtown Waterford," Darlene responded.

"I better get back in the kitchen and get things ready for dinner. Are we done, Hon?"

"I guess so," Frank said, "unless you have any more theories."

"That's all for today; come back tomorrow — fried shrimp special ... all you can eat. Seven ninety-five."

CHAPTER 30

Detective Roscoe Barnes was in the process of looking into the backgrounds of officers of Allied Manufacturing when Allied's chief counsel, John Pendergast, phoned him. His first impression of Pendergast had not been positive.

"Detective," Pendergast began, "I am able to answer your questions about what we paid Mr. Kincaid to acquire his company and the financial arrangement we had with him as our senior consultant. I hope you appreciate that it is appropriate and lawful to keep these matters confidential for competitive reasons."

Barnes, pleasantly surprised by the callback, did not interrupt.

"We paid Mr. Kincaid eighty-five million for everything — equipment, patents, and the building. It was an all-cash transaction. He did not receive any Allied stock.

"As to his consulting arrangement, we agreed to pay him five hundred thousand for each of two years.

"I hope this is responsive to your request."

It was, but Barnes took a few seconds to respond. "Yes, thank you, Mr. Pendergast. One additional question: since Mr. Kincaid was killed early on in his two-year consulting agreement, does the company's obligation end at the time of his death or extend out for the full two years?"

No response for, perhaps, five or ten seconds, but Barnes could hear a shuffling of paper. "It terminated with Mr. Kincaid's passing."

"I do have one more question, Mr. Pendergast. Did Mr. Kincaid's compensation package include any perks ... things like life insurance, stock options, medical coverage."

"Only medical."

Barnes felt he had what he needed. "I appreciate your getting back to me. My thanks to Mr. Donaldson, as well."

He hung up and, leaning back in his well-worn desk chair, closed his eyes and rubbed his forehead. Damn, he thought, I'm not used to getting such cooperation. Then he focused on the answer to his follow up question, the one about whether the consulting agreement ended at the time of Kincaid's death. That could be important. It saved the company from paying most of the one million bucks it would have paid Russell over two years. Was that enough of an incentive to snuff out the guy?

Barnes looked at his watch. Eight forty-five. Spence Atkins and Frank Wharton would probably still be in their morning meeting.

"Good morning, Frank. Is Spence with you?"

"Good morning. Yes. Let me put you on the speaker."

"I just hung up from a call with the chief legal honcho at Allied."

"Yeah?" Spence said.

"He gave me the figures I asked for and then some. I thought I might have to go to court but, bless his heart, here's what he said: all cash, eighty-five million for the company; five hundred thousand to Kincaid for each of two years as a consultant; and, listen to this, the consulting obligation terminated with his death, so they barely touched that commitment."

"Jesus!" Spence reacted. "Maybe we've been looking in all the wrong places for the killer. Maybe we should have been looking in Cleveland rather than little old Waterford."

"I don't know," Barnes replied. "But, at the very least, we need to dig deeper into Allied. I'm in the early stages of finding out all I can about the people in management and the directors on its board. I'll keep you posted.

"Oh, I almost forgot. The only perk Kincaid got was medical insurance. No stock options or life insurance.

"Anything new in West Virginia?"

Spence spoke first. "I spent some time with Florence Treadwell, the former assistant to Kincaid's father — the one Russell demoted. She's firm in her belief no one in Waterford did the crime and, as we talked, she picked up on a couple of my questions and embraced the idea that Allied didn't want Russell. She's very defensive of the plant manager, Jake Walter. So, bottom line, no significant addition to what we already think we know."

"And I visited with Darlene," Frank said. "She's the owner of the diner here in town. It and the local bar are the places where people talk freely. Darlene is a piece of work. Waterford doesn't need a newspaper or radio or tv for local news. Just talk with Darlene. She knows most everything. She's one step ahead of the rest of us most of the time. Anyway, she and Jake Walter are pals, and they'd talked the previous evening, so she played back to me his theory that Allied had Russell killed and deposited in our river. I didn't react."

"Maybe we ought to put this Darlene on retainer," Barnes said.

"Yeah," Frank replied with a chuckle. "Except she doesn't want us to solve this one if it's local; only if it's in Ohio. And, even then, she wouldn't mind if the perp got away with it. She doesn't feel an ounce of sorrow for Russell Kincaid."

CHAPTER 31

Florence Treadwell hadn't told anyone about the contents of the manila envelope addressed to her that she had found when she and Agnes Carney were going through the company's personnel files to search for any firings or disciplinary actions in recent years. Detective Spence Atkins had directed them to conduct the search as part of the investigation into Russell Kincaid's death.

The envelope was marked, "Florence Treadwell" and directly underneath her name, in upper case letters, were the words: "CONFIDENTIAL — FOR YOUR EYES ONLY." Junior Kincaid, who trusted Florence implicitly, sometimes used these markings for the most confidential of company matters. And, on occasion, the contents even dealt with family issues.

Upon discovering this unopened envelope in her own personnel file, she tucked it back into the folder and put it in her briefcase. She intended to open it in the privacy of her apartment that night but, amid all the turmoil surrounding the closing of the plant, she forgot about it.

Then, several evenings later, just as she was about to get ready for bed, she remembered it.

Opening the outer envelope, she found a slightly smaller, sealed one inside. This one stated, in Junior Kincaid's handwriting: "To be opened after my death."

A chill ran up Florence's spine and she could sense her eyes tearing. Pausing for a moment, her hand shaking a bit, she slit open the envelope. There was a handwritten letter from Junior attached to a several-page, typewritten document.

Drawing a deep breath, she began reading the handwritten cover letter. Junior's handwriting was difficult for anyone unfamiliar with it. The letters were jammed together, slanted steeply to the right and punctuation sometimes forgotten. But Florence had mastered the translation years before. It was dated March 10, 2016, a month prior to Junior's accidental drowning.

"Dear Florence,

As you know, I continue to be concerned that Russell doesn't seem to have his heart in the business and may not wish to carry it forward as you and I have. We should have plenty of time to determine his intent and ability because, the Good Lord willing, I expect to continue working for another ten or fifteen years.

Still, after giving the subject considerable thought, I have prepared the attached document. Should the circumstances summarized below and described in more detail in the attached document come to pass, I want you to deliver them to Michael Obitz, my long-time friend and family attorney, in Charleston.

These are my instructions as sole owner of Kincaid Fabricators.

1. Upon my death and assuming my only son, Russell, survives me, 100 percent of the ownership of Kincaid Fabricators shall pass on to him.

2. If Russell sells Kincaid Fabricators, 100 percent of the net proceeds shall pass on to him.

3. If, however, Russell sells Kincaid and subsequently dies without a direct heir, that portion of the net proceeds from the sale which is still definable and available shall pass on to the Town of Waterford, to be used as its citizens decide.

The necessary legal detail to accomplish these wishes is set forth in the attachment and will make sense to Michael Obitz or to whomever he assigns this matter.

As I know you appreciate, my father and mother, and Elizabeth and I have always had a deep affection for this town and its people.

Thank you, my dear Florence, for all that you have done for the Kincaid family, for our company, and, most assuredly, for me.

Warmest regards
Jeffrey R. Kincaid, Jr."

Florence had not slept well since reading the letter; nor had she passed it on to Obitz, as Junior Kincaid directed. She wasn't sure why she hadn't. Try as she might, she wasn't herself. She had experienced brief bouts of depression in the past but nothing like what she was feeling now. Maybe she feared the police would conclude she engineered Russell Kincaid's murder since she, and she alone, was aware of his father's instructions should Russell die after selling the company.

That Junior Kincaid wanted Waterford to benefit from the sale of the company now that Russell was deceased would be a wonderful surprise to the town. Although many of its citizens no longer had a job, there would be financial resources that might allow for new jobs to be created. Russell couldn't have squandered much of the proceeds because so little time had passed since the sale was finalized. So, why wasn't she uplifted by the good things that would result?

Enough, she said to herself, taking her phone from her purse and making an appointment with Obitz for the next day.

Michael Obitz, now in his early seventies, was universally respected in West Virginia legal and political circles. Much earlier, he had been twice elected Attorney General of the state. Many had encouraged him to run for Governor but, at the time, the financial responsibilities that go with supporting a family of six children, all of whom were expected to cycle through college, dictated he return to private practice. Establishing his own firm, he grew it over the years to become the largest in the state. Obitz, Fitzgerald, Clausen and Scott now had 130 lawyers specializing in areas like estate planning, corporate law including mergers and acquisitions, environmental law, and state and local government relations.

Florence gave herself a talking to on the drive into Charleston. She would be open in accepting the blame for not contacting Obitz sooner. She would explain she had initially forgotten about the envelope and then, upon reading its contents, became immobilized. She realized her delay would make things look worse in the eyes of the law. This was, after all, good news for a town that desperately needed some.

Obitz's office was on the top, eighteenth floor and his lawyers occupied all of several floors below.

Florence was ushered into a handsomely decorated conference room, its walls displaying a collection of watercolors devoted solely to the beauty of West Virginia's mountains and rivers.

"Florence," Michael Obitz's loud voice was both authoritative and warm. "How wonderful to see you. It's been too long. I meant to phone you when I heard about the plant closing. And, then Russell's death. How sad, how very sad. How are you?"

"I'm doing okay," she replied, though she wasn't.

"Did I somehow miss a memorial service for Russell?"

"No," Florence answered. "There was no public service in Waterford for obvious reasons. He was buried next to his mother and father in their private plot north of town."

"Well, good, I thought maybe I missed it. And, yes, I can see why nothing public would be done in Waterford. Now, what can I do for you?"

"I need your help," she said, her voice breaking ever so slightly. She handed Obitz the envelope.

"Before you open the one inside, I need to try to explain why I am delayed in bringing it to you."

She said her initial forgetfulness was likely caused by all that was going on at the plant and in town. But, she said she did not have a good reason for her subsequent delay.

Obitz opened the envelope and read Junior Kincaid's handwritten transmittal. Then he quickly examined the attachment, nodding as he paged through it.

"Florence, isn't this just like Junior? He was a wonderful, generous man. Now, don't you worry about the delay in getting this to me. I will make sure this is recorded properly and we'll get busy with locating and freezing the assets the community will be entitled to.

"Here's what we need to do. I will make State Police Superintendent Don Blackford aware of this and, if he says — as I believe he will — that his detectives need to interview you, I will accompany you to that interview. I am certain the State Police will agree to keep this information confidential as part of their investigation. For now at least, I believe that is in their interest as well as ours.

"Second, once we are able to locate and freeze the remaining net proceeds from the sale, we can, in consultation with the police, decide when and how best to communicate the information within the community. I know the people of Waterford are hungry for good news, but we need to wait until what I just described is pinned down. Specifically, we'll want to have a solid feel for how much money is at stake.

"Also, knowing, as you and I do, that Russell was very active sexually over the years, we will need to find out if he has fathered any children. If he has, we will need to know if he made any legal bequests that will compete with his father's stated wishes.

"We'll move as quickly as we can, but this is going to take some time. Have you talked with anyone else about Junior's letter?"

"No, sir. Absolutely not."

Justifiable

"Good. Again, don't worry about your delay. One, it hasn't been that much of a delay and, two, I don't see that it makes you legally vulnerable."

"You don't think the police will believe I had something to do with Russell's death?"

"No."

Florence heaved a sigh of relief. "I can't thank you enough. This whole thing has been so troubling, so heartbreaking. I'm just thankful Mr. Kincaid, Jr. didn't live to see all of this."

"So am I," Obitz said. "I will be in touch, probably in regards to a meeting with the detectives."

CHAPTER 32

Michael Obitz didn't waste any time in getting the legal and investigative wheels rolling.

He phoned Don Blackford, who he'd known for twenty-some years, and took him through what he had just learned from Florence.

"I expect your people will want to interview Miss Treadwell."

"Yes. Homicide Detective Spence Atkins, whom you know, and Frank Wharton, the Waterford police chief, have talked with her several times already, but they'll want to talk with her now that we know this."

"I told Miss Treadwell I would appear with her," Obitz said. "I assume you have no problem with that."

"None."

He then brought in three junior partners of the firm and, together they decided who would do what in terms of locating and freezing assets as well as determining if Russell, in a will or trust or any other legal document, had identified any heir or other beneficiary.

Don Blackford contacted Spence as soon as he hung up from his call with Michael Obitz. He took Spence through what he had learned from Obitz, and they agreed to try to set a meeting with Obitz and Florence for the next afternoon.

Spence said he wanted Frank in the meeting.

"I totally agree," Don said. "He's been a part of this from the start."

A call from Don to Obitz confirmed the meeting for two o'clock the next afternoon.

Spence phoned Frank to share what he had learned.

"I just got a call from Don. We have a meeting tomorrow at two in Charleston."

"What's that all about?"

"It seems that Russell's father wrote a note to Florence setting forth his wishes about ownership of the company."

"And ..."

"It was to go to Russell."

"We already knew that ..."

"But here's what we didn't know. If Russell sold the company and then died, the town would get whatever proceeds remained from the sale."

"Damn!" Frank said. "Russell didn't have but a short time between the sale and his death. He couldn't have spent much of it. That could be a substantial piece of change for Waterford."

"That's right."

✛ ✛ ✛

The five of them — Obitz, Don Blackford, Florence, Spence and Frank — met in Obitz's office.

Obitz passed out a copy of Junior Kincaid's hand-written letter and gave them a couple of minutes to read it.

"Excuse me," Frank said, "I just want to be sure I've got this straight. Now that Russell is dead, whatever remains from the proceeds of the sale comes to Waterford."

"Yes," Obitz replied, "unless there's some subsequent legal documentation out there that countermands it. We need to do a thorough search before we know for sure. It's possible — no, it's almost guaranteed — that something unforeseen will come up to delay the process. But, knowing what I know at this time, I believe Junior Kincaid's wishes will prevail.

"Now, gentlemen, I expect you have some questions for Miss Treadwell."

Spence started, "Miss Treadwell, why did you not tell us about this before now?"

Florence, shifting in her chair and occasionally rubbing her hands together, went through her initial forgetfulness and then said, "I really don't have a satisfactory answer. To be honest, I'm ashamed of myself. I knew I needed to get this letter and its attachment to Mr. Obitz, but maybe the pressure of all that was going on caused me to procrastinate. I am very sorry."

"To your knowledge," Spence continued, "did anyone at Kincaid — Russell or anyone else — know about this communication?"

"I feel certain they did not," she replied. "Both envelopes were sealed. I certainly did not know they existed until I found the outer envelope while doing the search with Detective Atkins' officers."

"Why didn't you turn the envelope over to the officers at that time?"

"Perhaps I should have but we were looking for files of employees who had been terminated or disciplined."

"Yes," Spence said, "and you were demoted and then terminated."

Florence paused for a moment. "At the time we were doing the search, everyone already knew I had been demoted. We didn't need to search the files to know that. We were searching for who else may have been terminated or disciplined in recent years prior to Russell's death."

"Did you remove your entire personnel file?"

"No, I left it in the file cabinet."

"So, why did you remove this particular outer envelope from that file?"

"Because of the written instruction on it — my name and the words, 'confidential, for your eyes only'. Clearly Mr. Kincaid Junior intended it for me and me alone."

Florence leaned forward. "Detective, I'm glad I removed it. If I hadn't, we wouldn't know what we know now: Mr. Kincaid, Junior's wishes. My only regret is that I did not bring this to Mr. Obitz sooner."

Spence turned to Frank. "Anything additional you want to ask?"

"No, I believe you've covered what I would have."

The meeting lasted about an hour, at which point Obitz said to Spence and Frank, "I will be representing Miss Treadwell. Feel free to phone me at any time you want to talk with Miss Treadwell or with me. Meantime, be assured my office will keep everything we have discussed today confidential as, I feel sure, you would want us to."

"Yes," Spence said. "We need to be kept informed on what your people find out about the money and about any directives Russell may have made. My officers will also be seeking answers to those questions. Maybe this double-teaming will accelerate the process."

"Sounds good," Obitz said. "Thank you, gentlemen. Thank you, Florence."

CHAPTER 33

Spence arrived the next morning a couple of minutes early for his daily meeting with Frank. Molly placed a carafe of coffee and a plateful of doughnuts from Darlene's on the conference table.

"Well, now what do we think?" he said to Frank as he sat down and poured himself a mugfull.

"I'm at a loss."

"I'm troubled that Florence waited to get the letter to Obitz. Why wait?" Spence asked.

"Maybe she was afraid we'd figure she had something to do with the murder because she was the only one who knew about the letter and what it said. Or," Frank added, "maybe as she said, she was just unglued by Russell's sale of the company and everybody, including herself, losing their job."

Spence stared at the doughnuts in front of him and selected a maple-iced one. "I'm still having a problem believing that lady had anything to do with the killing."

"That's where I'm at. I'm leaning toward Jake Walter. And we still have the possibility that Russell was done in by the good people at Allied."

"Yeah," Spence replied. "I'll check with Barnes to see if he's come up with anything."

"And I'm going to visit with the owner of the Roadside Bar again to see if he's hearing anything."

+ + +

Spence's call to Roscoe Barnes in Cleveland failed to produce much of anything. John Pendergast, the company lawyer, had narrowly escaped being disbarred ten years earlier for some shady transactions. But, they were unrelated to Allied.

Alfred Donaldson ran another company about fifteen years earlier that filed for bankruptcy. But other than that, he and the rest of the company's officers and directors checked out.

"We learned something here yesterday," Spence said, and he proceeded to take Barnes through what was discussed at the meeting with Michael Obitz.

"You think Miss Treadwell isn't telling us everything she knows?"

"I don't know. I'm going to give it a day or two and then go back at her. She didn't pull the trigger. I'm sure of that. But it's possible she knows who did, and, I suppose, it's also possible she orchestrated the whole thing.

"Meantime, Obitz's team of young lawyers is going to be checking to see if Russell Kincaid had any children we don't know about and what, if any, beneficiary designations he may have made."

Barnes didn't say anything more right away. "Assuming the son didn't mess up his father's wishes, it sounds like Frank's little old town, at some point, is going to get some good news."

"That's what it looks like," Spence replied. "This could be my first homicide case in all these years with a happy ending."

Justifiable

To Augie Martino's surprise, Frank asked the bar owner to come to the office for another talk.

"What are you hearing?" Frank began.

"Nothing new, really" Augie replied. "More of the same. Lots of talk about who might have done it. Still lots of anger about the closing and a lot of talk about Russell getting what he deserved."

"What about the two knuckleheads you steered me to? What are they saying?"

"They're not as loud as they were. Maybe you scared them a bit."

"You said there was lots of talk about who might have done it. What names have you heard?"

"Un," Augie paused, "the one I've heard the most is Jake Walter."

"Anyone else?"

"Russell's ex-wife. That's it. You gonna solve this thing," Augie asked.

"Time will tell. Keep your ears open and give me a call if you hear anything."

Augie, feeling a touch of pride that Frank Wharton, Waterford's top cop, was asking for his help, said he would.

CHAPTER 34

Ella Mae walked into Darlene's about 15 minutes earlier than usual, so neither Wally nor Phil was there yet. She exchanged greetings with Dagwood and paused briefly on her way to the booth Darlene faithfully saved for them every Saturday, Tuesday and Thursday to high five a couple of guys she knew from the plant.

"Frank hasn't arrested you yet?" one of them asked.

"Not yet. He's busy checking you out," she snapped back in her distinct cackle.

Darlene followed her, coffee carafe in hand.

"Good morning, Sunshine."

"Go to hell."

"Move over a minute," Darlene said, poking Ella Mae on the shoulder. " What's the latest?"

"You're asking me? Hell, girl, you're the one who knows everything. What do you hear?"

Darlene looked around to make sure no one else could overhear her. "Some lawyer types are checking out what Russell did with all the money he got from the sale. And, get this, they're also looking for any kids he might have fathered."

"I'm not surprised; I'd expect Frank is doing the same thing. 'Follow the money,' isn't that what they say in some of those political investigations on tv?

"I'd be surprised if there isn't a love child or two somewhere out there. Russell never struck me as someone who gave a lot of thought to using condoms. What else do you know?"

"Jeez," Darlene rose up from the booth, "you're always wanting more. Damn, I give you my best stuff and get nothing in return."

Wally and Phil came in together, passing Darlene as she headed for the kitchen.

"Morning, Beautiful," Wally said.

"Thank you, Hon. Her Majesty is already seated. She isn't saying much this morning."

"Jeez," Phil said, "she must be sick."

"You sick?" Wally asked, sliding in across from Ella Mae.

"No, I'm not sick. Is that what Ditzy Darlene said?"

"She just said you were quiet," Phil said, "so we assumed that meant you were sick."

"I'm fine, damn it. I'm just tired of the same old conversations three days a week with you two illiterate hillbillies."

"Whew, Philly Boy, she's okay. Everything's normal. She's just as mean and cantankerous as ever," Wally said.

"Screw you," Ella Mae said with a smile.

"I know one thing," Phil said, "I'm ready to go back to work. I've picked up a few handyman jobs around town, but they're not enough to pay the bills. What the heck are we going to do around here? Everybody go on welfare?"

"I still think there's a chance someone will buy the plant," Ella Mae said. "I don't know who or what they might put in it but, damn, it's too good to be left just sitting there."

"It better happen soon," Wally said, "or people are going to leave town and before long we'll look like one of those depressed coal mining towns no one gives a damn about."

"I expect our fearless mayor is doing his best to try to come up with something." Ella Mae said.

"I sure hope so," Phil said, unfolding his napkin as breakfast arrived and Dagwood was heard saying "Bye, Darlin'" to some departing customers.

CHAPTER 35

Armed with Allied's asking price, Mayor Steve Insley contacted the state Economic Development people in Charleston.

They had already been in discussions with Allied and suggested the asking price was too high given the economic conditions in the state and the availability of other buildings. Allied said it wanted to stick with the asking price but indicated it would be willing to negotiate with any qualified prospect.

Insley was encouraged that the state might provide a grant for, perhaps, three hundred thousand toward purchase of the property, but that likely would leave about a million five to come up with. Waterford didn't have anything close to that kind of money. And, even if it did, who could be enticed to move their business to Waterford and create the jobs it so desperately needed.

He did have a modest-sized fund he'd use to market the plant, emphasizing not only the physical facility but the skilled labor force within the community. He'd follow up with contacts made by the state and, in the interest of getting a deal done, he'd stay in touch with Al Donaldson, Allied's president.

The ideal would be to attract the kind of company or companies that would hire most of the people who had been terminated and pay them wages comparable to

Kincaid's. But, Insley realized, that was a long shot — not impossible, but improbable. More likely was converting the plant to a distribution center.

Waterford's location offered several advantages: a skilled, stable work force; Interstate highway access; an active rail line; and proximity to eastern and mid-western markets. Also, while attitudes may have changed as a result of the Kincaid fiasco, it was not a "union town."

The more Insley thought about the prospects, the more optimistic he became.

CHAPTER 36

Frank had given Spence Atkins the phone number for Beverly Kincaid. She agreed to meet with Spence and requested he come to her house.

"Ms. Kincaid, I know you have talked with Chief Wharton two or three times, and he has filled me in on those meetings. We appreciate your cooperation."

"You're welcome but, as I told Frank, I've had only a couple of brief conversations with my ex-husband since the divorce and none over the past year. So, I'm at a loss to know how I can help in any way."

The next fifteen or twenty minutes were spent rehashing what Frank had asked and how she had responded. She was consistent; no contradictions or expansions.

Then Spence turned to the couple subjects she hadn't been asked about — the subjects discussed at the meeting a day earlier in Michael Obitz's office.

"I appreciate my next question may be sensitive, but I need to ask it. Do you know if Mr. Kincaid fathered any children?"

Beverly took a breath, then said, "I honestly don't know. If he did, I'd probably be the last to know." She shook her head. "I wouldn't be surprised."

"When you were married, did you and your husband argue over any unexplained expenses?"

"Every married couple argues over money, don't they?" she replied.

"Yes, that's right. But my question dealt with expenses your husband may not have been able to explain."

The subject was uncomfortable for Beverly, but then she responded. "Yes, Detective. In fact, that was the first indication I had he was being unfaithful. I was naive at first. We'd been together since high school. I didn't want to believe he was doing the things he was doing. I didn't want to believe our marriage meant so little to him. I loved him — until I couldn't any more. He lied and lied, and then, toward the end, he didn't even bother to lie."

"So, he was paying prostitutes?"

"Yes. He finally admitted he was. But he also spent lavishly on dinners. And he shopped at jewelry and women's stores for things I never saw."

Spence didn't interrupt. Beverly was unloading.

"I don't know the names; I don't want to know. I'm trying to move on. It's not all that easy in a small town. I'm tired to death of people coming up to me, saying how sorry they are. I know that sounds ungrateful, but I've got to put all that unhappiness behind me and I can't do it with all the constant reminders — however well-intentioned they are."

Spence had made a note at the Obitz meeting to ask Beverly what law firm Russell used at the time of their divorce.

"Do you know what law firm your ex-husband used for things like estate planning, wills, things like that?"

"He used Sherman Wilson in Parkersburg during the divorce," she replied.

"Did he use anyone else for other legal matters?"

"Not that I know of. We went to college with Sherman. He and Russell were very close. I doubt he used anyone else.

"I haven't talked with Sherman since the divorce. He was on one side; I was on the other. I know he had to represent his client's interests, but he knew how Russell had destroyed our marriage. So, we don't talk anymore.

"I can give you his number ..."

"I'd appreciate that," Spence replied.

"Thank you for your cooperation. I realize Mr. Kincaid's death has caused you to relive things you are trying to move beyond. I'm sorry to have to put you through this, but we have a crime to try to solve."

"I do appreciate that, Detective. As I said to Frank, this town needs to know the answers, however uncomfortable they may be."

Spence dialed Sherman Wilson's number seconds after getting into his car.

Told that "Mr. Wilson is in court today," Spence asked when he would be back in the office."

"We expect him after four. May I have him call you?"

"No, I will come to your office."

There was a pause before another person got on the line.

"Mr. Wilson is in the middle of a trial. He won't ..."

Spence interrupted. "I am Chief Detective Spencer Atkins of the State Police. I need to see Mr. Wilson today. I will be there at four." Call ended.

Arriving a couple of minutes early, he handed the receptionist his card. "I have an appointment with Mr. Wilson."

"Please have a seat." She excused herself and walked through double doors, closing them behind her. Returning, she said, "Mr. Wilson will see you in a few minutes. He just returned from court."

Spence shuffled through The Wall Street Journal while he waited. The office was functional, not plush like Michael Obitz's.

Ten minutes later, a strikingly attractive woman emerged from behind the closed doors to say, "Mr. Wilson can see you now."

Seeing how well-dressed Wilson was, Spence didn't doubt he had been in court. Pin-striped navy blue suit, pale blue shirt, and blue, red and gray paisley tie — appropriate professional attire for appearing before a judge.

"Detective, Sherman Wilson. How can I help you?"

"I'll get right to the point, Mr. Wilson. I am investigating the death of Russell Kincaid ..."

"One of my best friends," Wilson said. "A tragic loss."

"And you are his lawyer, right?"

"I represented him in his divorce."

"Have you represented him in any way since then?"

"I did a bit of work in connection with his sale of the business."

"A bit? That was a big transaction. Wasn't it?"

"Yes, but another firm that specializes in mergers and acquisitions was the lead; I played a relatively small part."

"Did you represent Mr. Kincaid in any suits or settlements?"

Wilson noticeably grimaced at the question. "Detective, I am in the middle of a trial. I have a meeting with my client this evening. Can your questions wait?"

"No, Mr. Wilson, I'm sorry. They can't."

"How long do you think this will take, Detective?"

"I'd say no more than an hour ... for this initial session."

Wilson thought but didn't say, 'initial session'? Good God; just what I need.

Turning to his phone, he said to whomever answered, "Move my appointment back an hour."

Spence resumed. "You and Russell Kincaid were longtime friends."

"Yes. Ever since college."

"He admitted to paying hookers, to having extra-marital affairs ..."

Wilson interrupted. "Detective, I know you are familiar with attorney/client privilege ..."

"Very well aware, Mr. Wilson, but what I just said is a matter of record. Did you represent him in any claims or settlements?"

Wilson, uncomfortable from the start of this unscheduled meeting, didn't like the direction it was heading.

"Yes. But we're getting into privileged matters, Detective."

"I remind you," Spence said, "there is a murder that needs solving. The victim was your good friend and client. I am looking for the killer. I'm sure you want me to be successful. My questions are all aimed at achieving that.

"Tell me about the settlements. Did they concern women with whom Mr. Kincaid had had a relationship?"

"Yes."

"And how many such instances are we talking about?"

Wilson paused, shifting in his chair. "Three."

"That's it? That's all?"

"Yes."

"I need some specifics."

"All three dealt with paternity allegations."

"So, were the children born?"

"No. The pregnancies were aborted."

Wilson looked at his watch and fidgeted in his chair.

"So, he paid for the abortions. What else?"

"The women also got a cash settlement."

Spence asked when these settlements occurred. Wilson thought for a couple of seconds.

"I'll have to check."

"Okay, you can get that to me tomorrow. But can you approximate the dates now?"

Wilson rubbed his forehead. "The first was six or seven years ago. The second was maybe five years ago, and the third was, I believe, about three years ago."

"All while Mr. Kincaid was still married?"

"Yes. Anticipating your next question, Detective, no, I cannot provide their names. Confidentiality was agreed to as part of the settlement."

Spence chose not to squeeze Wilson harder on this point at this time. "Okay, you said none of these resulted in childbirth; all were aborted. Did Mr. Kincaid father any children that survive today?"

"Not to my knowledge. No."

"And you would probably know, right?"

"I believe so. Yes."

"Mr. Wilson, I know you and I are going to need more time together, so I'll ask just a few more questions today. When did you last see or talk by phone with Mr. Kincaid?"

"I saw him the week between Christmas and New Years and I talked with him in late January."

"What was his mood?"

"He was happy. He was getting settled in Cleveland. He liked the people at Allied."

"Did he have a will, a trust, something along those lines?"

"He'd had one with Beverly, but it was revoked as part of the divorce settlement."

"Had he done a new one? There was a lot of money at stake?"

Wilson briefly closed his eyes and slowly shook his head, "I don't believe so. I had been bugging him to do one. But, at least until recently, he didn't have anyone he wanted to designate as a beneficiary. I know it's crazy he didn't let me draft at least something because, as you said, a lot of money is involved. He kept telling me he had to close the deal with Allied; then he'd get with me on the personal stuff."

"One last question for today," Spence said. "You said he didn't have anyone to designate as a beneficiary until recently. Who are you referring to?"

"He was in a relationship with Elise Fortney. She's a great gal. A positive influence on him. I believe he wanted to take care of Elise."

"Anyone else?"

"I don't think so."

"I appreciate your talking with me, Mr. Wilson. I'll have additional questions and will be in touch."

CHAPTER 37

Spence called his boss, Superintendent Don Blackford, at home. He'd wait until morning to fill Frank Wharton in on his meetings with Beverly Kincaid and Russell Kincaid's attorney/friend, Sherman Wilson.

"I just had two, back-to-back interesting meetings. I say, interesting, because I struck it rich in terms of raw information. Time will tell whether any of it helps us solve the crime."

"I'm listening," Blackford replied.

Spence told him what Beverly had said about Russell's spending on other women, prostitutes included. He said he had no reason to doubt anything she said. "You and I have been in this business long enough to trust our gut on at least a few things. This woman, Beverly, had nothing to do with Russell's death. She's still affected by what he did, but she's doing her level best to move on.

"Now, here's where we struck it rich. She gave me his attorney's name and number. I just left his office."

"And ..."

"Okay, some highlights. Russell settled three paternity claims. No childbirths. All three aborted. Abortions paid for plus an amount to never talk about them."

"Jesus, didn't he ever hear about condoms?"

"That's not all. As far as Wilson knows, Kincaid hadn't gotten around to doing a will or trust. He'd had one when he was married but that went out the window with the divorce. So, unless he drew up something with another attorney, which Wilson doubts, he died without one."

Don didn't say anything for a few seconds. "So, unless someone else steps forward, it sounds like a lot of money might be headed toward Waterford at some point. Did he identify the women Russell paid off?"

"No. Part of the agreement was they'd keep their mouth shut. We can probably find a way to get to them but I doubt they'd provide anything useful. The payments were made as long ago as six or seven years and as recently as three — all while Russell was married. So, I don't see any linkage to the murder."

"Well, you did have an interesting day. Pretty good work, my friend. I'll call Mike Obitz in the morning and bring him up to speed. Maybe his guys will have come up with some of the same stuff or, hopefully, something additional. And you need to fill in Barnes in Cleveland when you get a few minutes. I'll be interested to know what, if anything, he's come up with."

Spence said he'd told Wilson he'd have additional questions. "Apparently, the guy is in the middle of a trial, so I might give him a day or two, but I'll bet he and Russell talked about the threats, maybe about the plant manager Russell didn't like. So, I'll follow up. Beverly Kincaid told me Russell and Wilson were close, and he confirmed that ... said he'd seen Russell over the Christmas holidays and talked with him as recently as late January. That's all I got for now."

"You earned yourself a drink," Don said.

"I'm minutes away from one. Talk with you tomorrow."

CHAPTER 38

Spence gave Frank a detailed briefing of his conversations with Beverly Kincaid and Sherman Wilson.

"Damn," Frank responded. "Three women; three abortions; three payouts. That boy was a loose cannon, excuse the pun. My daddy always said, 'If you're gonna play, you gotta pay.'"

"Well," Spence said, "he played and he sure as hell paid ... eventually, the ultimate price.

"I'll call Roscoe Barnes and fill him in. Also, we need to know where things stand with his part of the investigation. I still believe it's quite possible our friends at Allied arranged the killing."

Frank nodded agreement.

"And," Spence said, "we need to think about getting a warrant to at least get Jake Walter's computer and cell phone. Do you think we ought to think about doing the same with Florence Treadwell?"

"I don't think so. Let's see what more you get from Russell's lawyer, from Barnes and, when you're ready, from Jake. Jake may open up a bit more once he's hit with a warrant."

"Or, we risk it having the opposite effect. He gets a lawyer and clams up," Spence said. "We don't have to decide this right away."

Spence had planned to give Sherman Wilson, Russell's lawyer, a day or two before contacting him again. He wanted what they'd discussed to sink in. Wilson had been reticent but also helpful at their first meeting.

He didn't have to wait. Wilson phoned him the following afternoon, when Spence was in his office in West Charleston.

"Detective, I was just served papers alleging Russell has a living child, and the mother is making a claim on his estate on the child's behalf. I thought I should call you. I just got the paper fifteen minutes ago. I believe the claim is fraudulent. As I told you yesterday, I feel certain I would know if Russell had any heirs."

"I appreciate your calling. Can you have your secretary scan the papers and send me a copy on my phone?"

"Yes. Right away."

"Is your case still in court?"

"Yes. We should wind up tomorrow."

"We need to talk some more. How's four tomorrow afternoon?"

"It should be fine. I'll phone you only if things drag on and I cannot do four."

"Sounds good."

Spence leaned back, hoisted both feet onto the edge of his desk and mumbled to himself, "I would've bet a thousand bucks someone would step forward." The publication of legal death notices often stimulated a mixture of legitimate and bogus claims.

The claim appeared on his phone: Filed in Huntington ... mother, Julia Jamison ... child, Richard Jamison (no middle name provided) ... birth date, June 6, 2013. So, young Richard would be four in a few months.

Spence wasn't supposed to take sides but he couldn't help hoping the claim was bogus. If it was legit, that could get in the way of Waterford getting the money, and that town deserved a break.

He punched in Don Blackford's number.

"Yes, Spence, what's going on?"

"What I was pretty darned sure would happen, just happened."

"Yeah?"

"A woman has entered a claim on behalf of a child she says Russell fathered."

Spence took Don through what the filing said.

"Here's what I'm going to do," Don said. "Without telling Mike Obitz what we have, I'm going to ask what his guys have come up with. Since Mike indicated he is representing Miss Treadwell, and since Miss Treadwell may become a suspect, I need to be selective with what information we provide. You got most, if no all, of what they might come up with from your visit with Wilson. But, who knows, they may have picked up something we don't have. Meantime, you try to reach the woman making the claim."

Unable to find Julia Jamison's number, Spence phoned the lawyer identified on the claim, A. J. Washington.

A man answered the phone.

"Mr. Washington?"

"Yes, who's calling?"

Spence identified himself and briefly stated why he was calling.

"Mr. Washington, I need to talk with your client ... today.

"Detective, I doubt I can arrange it for today ..."

"Mr. Washington, it really needs to be today."

"Okay, sir, I will try to reach my client."

It was not absolutely essential the meeting be that day, but Spence always sought the optimal; he'd settle for second-best if he had to. He found it interesting Washington answered the phone himself; that probably meant his firm was small, maybe just himself.

While awaiting a callback, Spence phoned Roscoe Barnes in Cleveland to bring him current on what he had learned and see what, if anything, Barnes had to report.

Being told that Russell had paid for three abortions and a fourth woman had come forward with a paternity claim, Barnes' response was, "Damn, that young man was lucky he wasn't shot earlier."

Barnes said he had talked with Elise Fortney, who was working as a secretary in the president's office at Allied now that her old boss and lover, Russell, was history. He'd also talked with several individuals who, he was told, had been working closely with Russell on integrating Kincaid's business into Allied.

And, he'd gone through additional financial and ownership statements publicly-traded companies like Allied file with the regulators. "Nothing out of the ordinary," he said, "but those guys sure pay themselves well. I see where Alfred Donaldson got nearly three million bucks last year and Pendergast got a bit over two.

On top of that, they granted themselves a chunk of stock options."

"Maybe we should have chosen a different line of work," Spence said.

"Yep. Life would have been a lot simpler. No house payments, no car payments. But, hey, think of all the fun we have."

"I'll try to remember that, Roscoe, when I'm paying the bills the first of the month."

Julia Jamison's attorney, A. J. Washinton, called Spence and said he and his client could meet in his Huntington office at three that afternoon.

Washington, an athletic looking, African-American, who appeared to be about forty, greeted Spence with a firm handshake.

"Detective, meet Julia Jamison."

She, too, was African-American, and, while rather plainly dressed, was striking.

Spence briefly went through his routine about leading the investigation into Russell's death. He directed his attention to Ms. Jamison as he talked, looking for how and at what times she might react to his words. No reaction of any significance so far.

"Ms. Jamison, how and when did you and Mr. Kincaid meet?"

She leaned forward, folded her hands in her lap, and focused directly on Spence. "About four years ago at a charity event in Huntington. I was on the organizing committee and he was one of the sponsors."

"And that led to ..."

"We talked and he asked for my number. He seemed like a nice guy — well-educated, interesting, sociable. I gave it to him and he called the next day. We went to lunch a few days later."

"Did you know he was married?"

"No, I did not."

"When did you learn he was?"

"After I told him I was pregnant." Her posture stiffened noticeably when she said that.

"How did he react to that news?"

"He asked me to get an abortion. He said he was not ready to be a father."

"And you said?"

"First I cried, but then I told him I could not agree to an abortion. It's against my beliefs. Besides, we had talked about getting married. He hadn't proposed but we had talked. I said I was going to have our baby.

"He said he would pay for the abortion and give me twenty thousand dollars."

"How did you respond?"

"Not well. I was furious; he made me feel like a whore. You know, sex for money. I lost it. I guess I became hysterical. Then he said he was married and he couldn't be seen as fathering a child with someone other than his wife. He had lied to me ... told me he was single and led me to believe he was in love with me.

"He said he was going to divorce his wife, and we could be together."

"I told him to leave. I don't remember exactly what he said then ... something like 'I'll call you when you've calmed down'."

"And did he call you?"

"A few days later. He tried to apologize, said he wanted to see me. And then he had the gall to ask if I had reconsidered his offer. I told him 'no' and hung up."

"Did you see him after that?"

"No. He called repeatedly at first. I didn't answer. Then, a couple of weeks later, I did answer. I told him not to call again. I told him I would go to the police if he kept harassing me."

"So, you had the child ..."

"Yes. As much as I hated Russell, I love my baby boy. He's my life; he's who I live for."

Spence paused before asking his next question. "Did you accept any money from Russell Kincaid?"

"Not a dime, Detective. Not a dime."

"But now you are making a claim against his estate."

"Not for me. Nothing for me. For our son. Anything gained will go into a trust for him."

"Are you in a position to prove that Mr. Kincaid is the father?"

Julia's lawyer, A. J. Washington, spoke up, "Yes, we are."

Spence changed the subject and asked if Russell had talked at all about his job and the people he worked with. Julia said he mentioned in passing that he would inherit the family business, and that it was successful.

Spence left believing Julia Jamison. She'd have to prove her claim, but he believed she could. He also left respecting her for being true to her beliefs.

CHAPTER 39

Spence sat in his car for a few minutes collecting his thoughts. He needed to brief his boss, Don Blackford, on his meeting with Julia Jamison and her lawyer.

"Boss," he said, "this thing is becoming a damn soap opera. Wilson, Russell Kincaid's lawyer, phoned me to say he'd just received a paternity claim."

"Why am I not surprised," Don said.

"I hear you," Spence continued, "I just left a meeting with the woman who filed the claim and her attorney."

"Hey, you're moving pretty fast, young man," Don said.

"Thanks for the 'young man' reference. Yeah, the young woman is named Julia Jamison. She lives in Huntington and has a little boy who, she said, is going on four. She said Russell is his poppa.

"I won't bore you with all the details except to say Kincaid tried to get her to abort the pregnancy ... said he'd pay for it and give her twenty thousand to keep her mouth shut. Sound familiar?"

"What a scumbag!"

"Yep. She refused and they stopped seeing each other. No contact after that. Her attorney said they can prove Kincaid was the father. I don't doubt it. Ms. Jamison said she doesn't want anything for herself, just for her boy."

Spence paged through his notes. "She said Kincaid told her he was going to inherit a business but didn't go into any detail. Oh, and of course, he told her he was single. Then he admitted to being married but said a divorce was in the works. Very wisely, she dumped him."

"I don't see that any of this gets us closer to finding out who shot Kincaid," Don responded. "It just reinforces what a God-awful person he was."

Don said he would provide this additional information to Michael Obitz because the claim could possibly complicate the wishes of Russell's father that proceeds from the sale of the family business go to the town if Russell had no legal heir.

The call ended with Spence saying he would brief Frank Wharton and meet again with Sherman Wilson, Russell's attorney.

"So far as I can tell," Spence said, "Wilson is about the only friend Russell Kincaid had. He may be the one who somehow steers us in the right direction."

Frank Wharton listened intently the next morning as Spence took him through his meeting with Julia Jamison and her attorney.

"And you came away believing her?" Frank asked.

"Yeah. And her attorney said they can prove Kincaid is the father."

"Damn, do you figure she might end up getting all the money that was going to go to the town?"

"I don't know. Like you, I don't practice law, I try to enforce it."

Frank shook his head. "What a friggin' mess." He didn't want anything to negate the clearly stated wishes of Junior Kincaid, Russell's father.

Spence told Frank he hoped to meet with Sherman Wilson, Russell's attorney, later in the day. "Since they were such pals, I bet Wilson will know something about Russell's disagreements with the plant manager, Jake Walter. And, whether he does or doesn't, I believe it's time to get a search warrant and grab Walter's cell phone and computer. I know his friends keep telling us he'd never go after Kincaid, but I'm not so sure. Maybe doing the search will give us a yes or no answer.

"Then," Spence continued, "just to be sure we're covering all the bases, I'm leaning toward going after the same from Florence Treadwell."

Frank held off responding for a few seconds. "What about Elise Fortney, Russell's secretary/bed partner?" he asked. "Her cell phone and computer might contain something she isn't telling us."

"Good idea. Maybe we go after all three."

Spence drove to Parkersburg to meet again with Sherman Wilson. Wilson had been helpful in revealing Russell Kincaid's paying for several abortions and informing Spence of the paternity filing.

He opted to open with some softball questions.

"Do you know A. J. Washington, Julia Jamison's lawyer?"

"Yeah, a little. Not well, though."

"How did he know to serve you with the Kincaid paternity claim?"

"My name was on the legal notice we published after Russell's death. Also, he knew I had represented Russell in the divorce and that proceeding, as you know, received a lot of local attention."

"So, am I right in concluding you are once again representing Mr. Kincaid?"

"Yes. Unless someone comes forward with a piece of paper signed by Russell that says they have the job."

"Good," Spence said, "that simplifies things."

Spence reminded Wilson he'd said, at their initial meeting, he didn't think Russell had fathered any children.

"That's right. I didn't think he had. I still question whether he did. I believe he would have told me; we worked together on the abortion settlements. He wasn't shy about those. Do they say they have proof?"

"That's what they say."

"I'll have to put that to the test."

Spence thumbed through his note pad. "Mr. Wilson, are there any other skeletons in your client's closet? This guy becomes more notorious each passing day."

Wilson couldn't restrain himself from smiling. "Not that I know of. But, because there's a lot of money in his estate, don't be surprised, Detective, if more claims of one kind or another come rolling in."

"Mr. Wilson, you said you were both a friend and attorney. Did Russell tell you anything about the people he worked with at Kincaid?"

Wilson leaned back, rubbed his chin a couple of times, and held off answering for a moment. "Some, yeah."

"Who, specifically?"

"He said he needed to move his father's assistant to another job."

"You mean Florence Treadwell?"

"Yes, that was her name."

Spence asked why, and Wilson said Russell told him he wanted to start with a clean slate. He wanted his own person in that job.

"Anyone else?"

"He wanted to get rid of the plant manager. I remember him saying that. We talked a bit about what kind of cash payment might need to be offered."

"You're referring to Jacob Walter?"

"Yes. Russell felt Walter had been in the job too long ... was resistant to change."

"So, why didn't he get rid of him?"

"It became unnecessary because the offer from Allied to buy the company came in at about that time."

Spence asked Wilson if he and Russell had talked at all about the effect the sale of the company would have on Waterford.

"Yes. He regretted that. But he was much less interested in the business than his father had been. This was a chance that probably wouldn't come along again — an all-cash offer; a large amount of money. It would free him up to do whatever grabbed his interest. Making fire hose valves wasn't his idea of excitement."

"Do you think he knew how much he would be hated?"

"He knew he'd need to leave town, and he wanted to do that anyway."

"Did you or he fear for his safety?"

"Not if he got out of town, no."

"Are you aware of any threats he may have received?"

"Yes. He told me of a few phone calls."

"Did he say who he thought was making the threats?"

Wilson said Russell didn't know but thought they may have been the work of Jake Walter.

"That's all I've got right now." Spence said. "Is there anything else you want to share ... anything else that might help me find out who killed your client?"

"No. You now know what I know."

"I appreciate your help," Mr. Wilson. "Call me if any more claims come in."

"I will."

CHAPTER 40

Spence decided the time had come to seek a court order to seize Jake Walter's cell phone and any computers he may have. Too many people had confirmed Jake and Russell didn't get along. Jake had denied knowing Russell planned to get rid of him, but Spence wasn't buying that.

He wasn't ready to charge Jake with anything. He needed evidence. Maybe those communication tools would provide some answers.

And, while he was at it, he'd phone Detective Barnes in Cleveland to ask him to seek an order to obtain Elise Fortney's cell phone and computer as well as any computer Russell may have had. Russell's cell phone was missing, along with the clothes he wore when he was killed.

"Not a problem," Barnes responded. I'll let you know what we come up with."

Spence decided to hold off seeking Florence Treadwell's communication devices. He'd wait to see what, if anything, he learned from Jake's and Elise's.

Two State Police cars, each with two officers, showed up at Jake Walter's house without any advance notice.

Caught totally by surprise, Jake became upset.

"Hey, I need both my phone and computer. I'm in the process of trying to find a job. I'm calling people; they're calling me back. What the hell am I supposed to do?"

"Mr. Walter," one of the officers responded, "all I can tell you is we need the phone and computer. Do you have a second computer?"

"No."

The whole process took about fifteen minutes.

As the police left, Jake's wife, Vivian, put her arms around him. "Jake, why are they doing this to us?"

"They think I killed Russell. I've cooperated every step of the way. This is crazy. The last thing we need at this time is the expense of hiring a damn lawyer, but I've got to get one. I'm not going to let them lock me up for something I didn't do."

They remained at the door, arms around each other, worried about what the future held.

The approach in Cleveland was just as abrupt. The police arrived unannounced that evening at the home Elise and Russell had been sharing and collected Elise's cell phone and computer and Russell's computer.

Elise was furious. "How dare you come busting in and taking these things. Don't you know this poor man was murdered? This is a violation of my rights ... and his."

The police went about their assigned responsibilities and left.

Minutes later, Elise was on the phone to Sherman Wilson.

"Sherm, the Cleveland cops just came and seized my phone, my computer and Russell's computer. What the hell is going on? They have no right to do that, do they?"

"Did they have a warrant?"

"Yes, but ..."

"They can do it."

"Did you know anything about this?" she asked.

"No. I have been contacted by West Virginia's finest. But, no, I did not know they were going to get Cleveland to come after your stuff."

"What are they after?"

"They're after Russell's killer. I can only speculate that they are looking for anything on any of those devices that might lead them in the right direction. They'll go through this pretty quickly and, assuming they find nothing of value, they'll get your phone and computer back to you. I wouldn't be surprised if they keep Russell's for at least the time being."

"That's an invasion of my privacy; can't we sue?"

"No, a court approved the seizures. There's no hidden agenda; they're just doing their job."

Elise didn't have any more questions and Wilson wasn't about to volunteer any information about the paternity claim. She was upset enough for one day.

CHAPTER 41

State Police Superintendent Don Blackford phoned Attorney Michael Obitz to see if Obitz's lawyers had located any documents that might interfere with Junior Kincaid's wishes that Waterford benefit from the sale of the company.

"Not a thing," Obitz replied. "So far, so good."

"Well, we're looking into something that might have an impact."

"Like what?" Obitz asked, frowning.

"There's been a claim on behalf of a child."

"You mean someone's saying Russell had a love child?"

"Yes. The child is going on four. Spence Atkins met with the mother and her attorney and they say they have proof."

"God damn! I shouldn't be surprised. Russell just couldn't keep his pants on. His dad and I talked about it. He messed up what should have been a wonderful marriage and he embarrassed his wife and his parents time and time again.

"Did Russell pay any child support or take any responsibility?"

"The mother says he offered to pay for an abortion and give her twenty grand. She told Spence she refused both, and the relationship ended. She said she even threatened to call us if he didn't stop harassing her."

"Do you think she's legit?"

"Spence does."

"Well. Unless there's some written commitment, I don't believe she's entitled to anything," Obitz said. "However, assuming they can prove the child was fathered by Russell, I might want to propose a payment of some amount."

"Spence said she doesn't want anything for herself; she wants it for the child."

Turning to another subject, Blackford asked, "Did your guys find out how much money Russell still had from the sale?"

"They're not finished searching, but it looks like it could be something north of seventy million. He was paid eighty-five. I'm not sure of the tax treatment because the money is going to a town."

"Wow! That's some serious money."

Spence had a few additional questions for A. J. Washington, Julia Jamison's attorney. No need to drive to Huntington, they could be handled by phone.

"Mr. Washington," Spence began. "are you in communication with Russell Kincaid's attorney?"

"Yes. I called him today to follow up on our claim."

"Have you had dealings with him in the past?"

"No."

"How did you know who to serve?"

"From the published notice."

"Did you contact Ms. Jamison or did she contact you?"

"I'm no ambulance chaser if that's what you're inferring. She contacted me."

"I'm not inferring anything, Mr. Washington. I'm asking straight-up questions."

"Okay, Detective, but I don't do that kind of stuff. You can ask anyone who knows me."

"Mr. Washington, I am well aware of attorney/client privilege, but is there anything — anything at all — you can tell me that might steer me toward Russell Kincaid's killer."

"Nothing. My client's only interest is as stated in our claim — that their son is entitled to a share of his father's wealth."

Spence didn't expect any help, but experience taught him to ask. He continued to believe that Washington and Ms. Jamison were telling the truth. Others would decide if they shared in Kincaid's estate. It wasn't his department; he was a homicide cop.

CHAPTER 42

Jake Walter got madder by the minute after the police took his cell phone and computer. He needed both. He had been busy seeking a job, and doing that was impossible without those tools. How in the hell could he explain not returning calls or answering emails? Tell them the cops seized them? Oh, sure, that would improve his prospects.

He knew he should contact an attorney but, before that, he'd drive to the Police Department and complain to Chief Frank Wharton. He knew he should reverse the order of those two things, but he was sufficiently pissed off, he'd see Frank first.

"Molly," Jake had known her since she was in high school, "I need to see the Chief." No hello. No how are you?

"Hi, Jake, have a seat. He's on the phone. I'll tell him you're here."

She closed the door after entering Frank's office.

Hanging up, Frank asked, "What's up?"

Jake Walter is out front and he needs to talk with you. He sure seems upset."

"Jake, come on in here," Frank said, opening the door. "What's on your mind?"

"Frank," Jake's voice rose a few decibels, "did you send the State Police to my house to scare the hell out of Vivian and take my phone and computer? Did you?"

"Jake, calm down. Take a breath. No, I did not. I don't direct the State Police to do anything."

Having said that, Frank put his arm around Jake.

"Jesus, Frank, two state cars roll up, four cops come charging in ... by now, I'm sure the entire town is convicting me of something I had absolutely nothing to do with."

"Jake, the state, with whatever help I can provide, is trying to solve a murder case. They're looking for anything and everything. You're not being singled out. Others will experience what you experienced."

"Yeah, but damn," Jake's voice lowered to a more normal volume, "I'm trying to find a job. I'm on the computer or phone a lot. What the hell do I do now?"

Frank thought for a moment. "I know Spence Atkins talked with you. He's in charge of the investigation. I'll ask him to do what he can to speed up the process of getting your stuff back to you."

"I'd appreciate that. Ever since Russell shut down the business, life around here has been hell. This was a great town, a great place to live. Now, everybody's on pins and needles.

"I sure hope you guys are checking out Allied. I think you're on the wrong track looking for the killer here. Sure, most of us ended up hating Russell. But you know us. You're one of us. We use our guns to hunt, not kill people. Before Russell, how many murders since you've been here? How many?"

"One," Frank answered.

"I've said it before. Allied got what it wanted in patents and equipment. It didn't need or want Russell. What a perfect idea. Pop him off and drop him in our river."

Frank let Jake unwind. "Jake, I can't say much because the investigation is ongoing but, be assured, the Cleveland police are involved."

That seemed to calm Jake more.

"I apologize for coming in here hollering," he said. "I'm under a lot of pressure. Not too long ago I had a good job, lived in a great little town, life was good. Now, I'm really at loose ends."

"Not a problem, my friend," Frank said. "Fielding complaints is part of my job description. Hey," he said, motioning to the plate on the edge of his conference table, "I can't eat all these doughnuts. And Molly just made a pot of fresh coffee. So, stay for awhile."

Jake stayed, and the conversation turned to deer hunting and the best kinds of bait to use in the river.

Frank phoned Spence Atkins a few minutes after Jake Walter left.

"I knew you were planning to go after Jake Walter's phone and computer, but I didn't know it had happened."

"Sorry," Spence said, "I should have told you. We got the warrants covering him, Elise Fortney, and Russell. I haven't yet requested authorization to go after Florence Treadwell's devices. But I plan to."

Then Frank told Spence he'd spent the last hour with Jake Walter, who was "as pissed off as I've ever seen him."

"I'm not surprised," Spence said. "But, as you know, we consider Jake Walter a person of interest and we need to know who he's been talking to or exchanging emails with."

"Yeah, I agree," Frank said. "Jake played back to me his belief that Allied knocked Russell off. The only thing I said was that Cleveland P.D. is involved."

"Good. And, as you know, I agree that's a real possibility. Barnes in Cleveland is on it, and he's a damn good cop."

Then Frank conveyed Jake's plea that his phone and computer be returned as soon as possible, explaining that Jake was dependent on both as he tried to get a job.

"I understand," Spence said, "I'll pass the word on. Assuming there's no evidence in either device, we ought to be able to get them back to him in a couple of days. I'll keep you posted.

"Oh, and while I have you, you may have read there was one homicide in Charleston the night before last and one in Huntington two days before that. I've got to get on both of those, so I'm not going to be coming your way for our morning meetings unless there's a special need. Our beautiful state still racks up about a hundred homicides a year, so my plate is never empty.

"I'll be sure to phone you if I learn anything of interest. You do the same. Call me anytime. I will be acquiring Florence's cell phone and computer, if she has one. Probably tomorrow or the next day.

"Tell Molly I'll miss her coffee and doughnuts."

CHAPTER 43

"This is getting a little old," Wally said as he slid into the booth at Darlene's where Ella Mae and Phil were already seated.

"You mean being in the company of Philly Boy and me?" Ella Mae asked.

"I mean the whole damn thing — not having a job to go to, not having a pay check coming in, not hearing back from anyone in response to my applications."

"Yeah, I hear you," Phil responded. "Nobody seems to be hiring."

"Well," Ella Mae said, "you two are sure fun to be with this morning. If it wasn't for Dagwood's always cheery mood, I'd be better off having a friggin' doughnut at home."

"You need any work done around your place, Ella Mae?" Phil asked. "I have a strong back and am pretty good at following directions."

"My garage looks like the county dump. You want to clear it out? Minimum wage plus a six-pack if I'm happy with the final product."

"Damn," Ella Mae, you're all heart," Wally chimed in.

Ella Mae smiled and gave him the finger.

"I'll be there tomorrow," Phil said.

Darlene was anxious to talk with her favorite threesome and, sensing a lull in other customers' needs, appeared.

"Move over, Hon," she said, poking Phil on his shoulder."

She was busting to share the latest. "The State Police grabbed Jake's phone and computer."

"Jeez," Wally said. "They're really picking on him."

"That's not all," Darlene said, "I think they'll be going after Elise's in Cleveland and Miss Florence's."

"How do you know all this crap?" Ella Mae asked.

"I have my sources, Missy."

"We know that," Phil said.

Satisfied she had fulfilled her responsibility as town crier, Darlene left to resume taking care of other customers' needs.

"I'm thinking they'll come after your phone," Wally said, looking at Ella Mae.

"If they do, all they'll find is hours of phone sex," she replied, causing Phil to temporarily choke on his orange juice.

"I hear the mayor is talking to the Economic Development folks in Charleston," Wally said. "He's doing what he can to try to get someone to put something in that building."

"I sure hope he succeeds and it's someone who will pay more than minimum wage. I don't have to get what I made at Kincaid. But it'd sure be good to get something close to that and not have to think about moving," Phil said.

"What about you, Ella Mae, you looking for work anywhere?" Wally asked.

"You mean other than selling my body?"

Phil let out a monster laugh, thankful it didn't coincide this time with a mouthful of juice or coffee.

"No, seriously," Wally asked.

"I haven't started looking yet. Ever since I divorced that deadbeat husband of mine, I've tried to save something from each paycheck. I've got a little money in the bank, so I'm okay for awhile. I could always waitress. That's what I did before I went to work at Kincaid. I was almost as beautiful then as I am now."

Phil just rolled his eyes, thinking how much he enjoyed this crazy woman's sense of humor.

"Damn it," Philly Boy, "stop rolling your eyes. You know it makes me dizzy," she barked.

"Dizzy, dizzy, dizzy" came the reply from the sage in the cage up front.

CHAPTER 44

Sherman Wilson knew all about former Attorney General Michael Obitz and his largest-in-the-state law firm, but had never talked with him until now.

"It's Mr. Obitz," Wilson's secretary said.

"Mr. Wilson, Michael Obitz."

"Yes, sir, Mr. Obitz."

"Forget the sir, and it's Michael or Mike."

"Yes, sir ... I mean Michael."

"We need to talk, Sherman. I'm involved in some work relating to Russell Kincaid's death. Am I correct in assuming you were his attorney up to the time of his death?"

"Yes. I did a fair amount of work for Russell. He didn't have me on a retainer or anything like that. But, as far as I know, I was the only attorney he worked with. And, as you may know, he was a good friend."

"I'm not at liberty to tell you much about why I am involved, but I need to ask you a couple of questions."

"I'll help if I can," Wilson replied.

"Did Russell have a will or a trust?"

Wilson remembered Detective Spence Atkins had asked the same question. "Not that I know of; the one I'd done for him a few years back was negated by his divorce settlement."

"You'd know if he had one, wouldn't you?"

"Yes, I think so. I had been bugging him about doing one even before he came into all the money from selling the company."

"I understand he may have had a child out of wedlock."

Knowing something about Michael Obitz's connections in the state and beyond, Wilson was only mildly surprised he knew this. "Yes. I was served papers a couple of days ago."

"What else can you tell me?"

"Not much. I don't know whether it's a legitimate claim or not. There will need to be a DNA match or some other definitive evidence. I'll be meeting with the woman's attorney tomorrow. Can you tell me, Michael, anything about why you are involved?"

"Not at this time. I wish I could and I will when I can."

Wilson and A. J. Washington met in Washington's office in Huntington. About the same age and having attended some of the same undergraduate classes at WVU, they opened by talking about football, a sport taken very seriously at their alma mater. Washington had played for the Mountaineers in his sophomore and junior years before blowing out his knee.

Washington was the first to turn to the claim. "My client has a legitimate claim and we're prepared to go to court, if we need to."

"A. J., as far as I can tell, Russell Kincaid had no will, no trust, no nothing. I'm in the process of confirming that. But I knew Russell well enough to be sure he would not leave any money to your client.

"I assume you have proof Russell fathered the boy?"

"Yes we do."

"I am in the early stages of trying to quantify Russell's estate. This may take a bit of time."

"Sherman, I want to be clear on this. I'm not trying to make my client filthy rich as a result of your client's death. We want to be fair. But we also feel strongly that Mr. Kincaid has a responsibility to the child."

"I appreciate your candor." Wilson didn't react but thought that maybe something could be worked out. Being a father himself, he silently agreed with what Washington had said.

Wilson promised to be in touch as soon as he was able to confirm the value of the estate and whether or not others stepped forward to enter claims.

They ended by agreeing the Mountaineers would have another strong year. That is, until they had to play Ohio State in Columbus.

CHAPTER 45

Florence Treadwell's little terrier, Petunia, barked like crazy whenever anyone came to the door.

"Hold just a minute," Florence called out, picking up Petunia and depositing her in the bedroom. Opening the door, she was surprised but not shocked to see two State Troopers.

"Miss Treadwell," one of them said, handing a sheet of paper to her, "we have been authorized by the court to collect your cell phone and computer."

"I don't know why anyone would be interested in either but my phone is in my purse and the computer is in the den. I'll get my phone; the den is the first door on the left. When will you be returning them?"

"I don't know, Ma'am. But there is a phone number on the form I gave you. I'd give it a day or two, and then call.

"Do you have any other devices, like an iPad?"

"No. I do not."

The officers left after spending no more than ten minutes in Miss Florence's apartment.

She took a few minutes to collect her thoughts before going into the kitchen to use her land-line phone.

"Molly? It's Florence. Is the Chief available?"

"Hold just a minute, Miss Florence."

"Hi, what's up, young lady?" Frank asked.

"State troopers just took my cell phone and computer."

"Well, Spence Atkins is gathering up stuff from several people. You can probably expect to get them back in several days. He's covering all the bases."

"Jake told me they grabbed his yesterday," Florence said. "They'll be bored to tears by what's on mine.

"You knew your friend, Detective Atkins, would be doing this?"

"Yes. But I can't be going around alerting people."

"No, no, I understand."

"Other than that," Frank asked, "anything else new?"

"No, if it weren't for the pain being felt by so many people in town, I'm finding I enjoy not having to go to work. For me, the fun and satisfaction there ended when Junior passed away."

"A lot of folks feel the same way," Frank said.

Rather than phone, Florence drove out to Jake Walter's. He was where she expected to find him: in the garage, door open, working on his "baby."

"Are you ever going to finish this thing?" she asked.

"Hi, Miss Florence. My goal is to have it fully restored in time for the July Fourth parade."

Like so many small towns across America, Waterford had a Fourth of July parade — everything from moms pushing strollers, kids riding bikes, scout troops marching, a fire truck or two, and antique and not-so-antique vehicles.

"Well," she said, "you will be happy to know that I, too, am now without my cell phone and computer."

Jake exhaled a strong breath. "I'll be damned. Well, I hope those guys enjoy themselves. As I told you, I marched into Frank's office prepared to give him all kinds of hell. He sort of implied that this is par for the course, and if they don't find something incriminating, we'll get our stuff back in a few days.

"Aside from feeling like my rights are being stomped on, I need both of my devices because I'm spending a bunch of time trying to find a damn job."

"Well, I just wanted you to know you're not alone in being investigated," Florence said.

"Thanks. Oh, I forgot to tell you, I lined up a lawyer. I hate going to that expense, especially when I'm not bringing home a paycheck. But, I'm beginning to believe they're coming after me. I didn't have a damn thing to do with Russell's death, but Frank and that Spence guy keep coming back at me."

"Well, for what it's worth," Florence said, "I told both of them more than once that you'd never do such a thing."

"Thank you, dear lady. I sure miss the times we had working for the company. Sour as I am right now, no one can take away the memories of those days."

Since it was early afternoon and she had to pass Darlene's on the way back to her apartment, Florence decided to stop for a glass of sweet tea, maybe a cup of soup. I think the soup for today is tomato basil, she thought. Darlene had a different soup for each day of the week. Monday was minestrone. Friday was clam chowder.

The sequence never changed. Customers seemed to like the predictability.

"Well," said Darlene as Florence walked through the door. "Lookie who's here." Darlene took Florence by the hand and led her to the far corner booth so they could have some privacy. "Let me say goodbye to that couple up front. They're about to leave. You want some tea?"

"That would be nice, and a cup of soup."

"Tomato basil, okay?"

"What if it isn't?" Florence teased.

"Then you're not having soup today, my dear."

The always attentive Dagwood picked up on the theme: "Soup today, soup today."

A couple of minutes later, the diner to themselves, Darlene returned with the tea and soup, and slid into the booth.

"I would have called you on my cell, but I can't," Florence said, smiling a bit.

"What do you mean you can't?"

"No phone; no computer."

Darlene's eyes widened. "You're not going to tell me the troopers took yours like they took Jake's?"

"Yes, they did."

"Mother of God! What are those people up to?"

"I just came from Jake's," Florence said. "He'd talked to Frank and he led Jake to believe they're just crossing the t's and dotting the i's. I guess they're looking for any activity around the date of Russell's murder. Some kind of linkage. I don't know. They're not going to find anything on either my phone or computer, I can guarantee that.

There's nothing but routine conversations and emails with friends like you."

Darlene didn't doubt anything her long-time friend, Florence, said.

"I think Jake's on the right track," she said. "Allied paid for a hit and whoever they paid shot the little prick and dumped him into our pristine Maplethorn so everyone would conclude one of us did it.

"It's time to leave West Virginians alone and get busy up in Cleveland. Harass those buckeyes for a while," Darlene said, pounding the table so hard that Florence's soup splashed over a bit.

"Sorry, dear, I get a little emotional."

CHAPTER 46

Mayor Steve Insley was determined to get someone to buy the Kincaid plant and hire at least a bunch of Waterford's skilled but unemployed workers. He didn't want to settle for minimum-wage jobs. These folks were proven performers. The highest of high tech was out of the question, but they could be retrained for most anything else.

That was part of his pitch to the state Economic Development Department. He'd worked with the EDD folks to develop a marketing brochure and website.

As a long-time member of the state Chamber of Commerce, he'd served on a number of committees and, in the process, made a lot of contacts. Each of them heard from Insley by mail, email, phone — maybe all three.

He succeeded in getting a meeting with the Governor for himself and several other Waterford business leaders. And, he sent out a mailing to metal fabricating companies throughout the East and Midwest. "Blanket bombing" is how he described the communications effort.

Ideally, one company would occupy the entire plant. But, with a relatively small amount of work, it could be divided into several distinct sectors. So, if it took two, three or four separate businesses to fill the space, Insley was okay with that.

No takers yet. But Insley wasn't going to let go until something good happened. Waterford wasn't going to go down. Not on his watch.

Spence phoned Frank as soon as he got the reports.

"Well, as we sort of thought would be the case, the phones and computers are clean. Nothing that leads us anywhere," he said.

"Any encouraging words from Cleveland?" Frank asked.

"No. Barnes is still doing his thing. If there's anything to be found, he'll find it."

"So," Frank said, "we're where we were several days ago."

"It looks that way. Are you picking up anything? Anybody saying anything we haven't already heard?"

"Nope. Folks are still pissed. But the shock is pretty much gone. Most everyone I talk with is busy trying to find a job. They're realistic. They don't expect anyone to come in overnight to buy the plant and hire everybody back. So, at least for now, they're cutting back on spending, planting bigger vegetable gardens, trying to sell stuff they don't need, and taking minimum-wage jobs if they can find them."

"Sturdy people," Spence observed.

"That's us. We're survivors."

Frank told Spence he wasn't planning to interview anyone else. "I'm just keeping my ear to the ground. Maybe, just maybe someone will say something they wish they hadn't. If they do, we'll be ready to pounce."

Spence agreed. "We talked about this early on. If the killer is local, our best chance to catch him is if he confides to someone or brags."

"You think we'll ever find Russell's car?" Frank asked.

"Very unlikely. Our only hope is if it was dumped in the river, and your river doesn't run that deep for miles up and downstream. But I doubt it's in the river. I expect it's been disassembled or is putting around somewhere in Mexico."

Then Spence got a bit philosophical. "I've been in Homicide for a long time. I'm an odd ball because I still like my job. It used to really get to me when I couldn't solve a crime, especially if the killer was the type that might do it again. But, I've come to realize I'm not going to solve every case. Some people are going to get away with murder. It's just a fact. So, I do my best. If I succeed, great. If I don't, well, I tried."

"You're thinking we might not solve this one?" Frank asked.

"I never give up. I'm just saying if we don't, it won't be the first and we shouldn't beat ourselves up."

"Spence, I made the decision some years ago I didn't want the kind of job you have. I'm happy being here in Waterford, and I'm sure as hell looking forward to getting this chapter over and done with."

"I hear you. We'll stay in touch."

This time it was an unmarked state car that pulled up in Jake Walter's driveway.

"Mr. Walter," the trooper said. "Here are the devices we borrowed. We apologize for any inconvenience we may have caused. We appreciate your cooperation."

"So, am I in the clear?" Jake asked.

"I'm sorry, sir. I am not authorized to discuss an investigation." The trooper turned, walked to his car and drove off.

Jake wanted to phone Miss Florence but doubted she had her cell phone back yet.

Minutes later, the same patrolman, saying the same things, delivered Florence's phone and computer to her.

Figuring Jake already had his phone, she punched in his number.

"I thought you'd call," Jake said.

"Well, I've got my stuff back," she said.

"Me, too. I hope I haven't missed out on some spectacular career opportunity."

"I hope not. I can be a little more relaxed about this whole process than you. You've got a family to support. I don't; it's just me. I'm not planning to go back to work. I'll stay active in the community. That'll be more than enough."

Anxious to have her phone and computer returned, Elise Fortney had been contacting the Cleveland P. D. each day for nearly a week.

"We'll contact you," she was told each time.

She was getting madder and more anxious each day. Her life had become a mess. She'd contacted Sherman

Wilson, Russell's lawyer, and was told Russell hadn't gotten around to doing a new will or trust. So the marriage and wealth she thought would be hers never materialized.

The house she and Russell had been renting was far too big and expensive for her. She guessed she'd stay in Cleveland. Having worked for and lived with Russell would make returning to Waterford difficult, to say the least. She needed to get busy breaking the lease on the big house and finding something she could afford.

Mourning Russell's death had been replaced with anger that he didn't provide for her. Reflecting back on their relationship, it was always all about him. He insisted she go along with what he wanted to do, when he wanted to do it.

Elise had chosen not to believe all the stories about his sexual escapades. And yet, down deep, she knew. She just hoped she could change him — make him happy. She had loved him, but now she didn't. She felt used. She felt neglected. And, she felt alone.

CHAPTER 47

Sherman Wilson, Russell's attorney, was now certain Russell had not gone to anyone else to draw up a new will and trust. And, while he didn't expect any legitimate claims to Russell's riches to come in, he was a bit surprised he hadn't received some of the other kind. All he had was the one from A. J. Washington on behalf of Julia Jamison.

It was unlikely a court would uphold that claim but it would have to be dealt with in some way.

He'd received a second call from the legendary Michael Obitz, asking about claims. He had told Obitz about the one claim in their initial conversation and said he'd be meeting the next day with the woman's attorney.

"How'd your meeting go?" Obitz asked directly, never one for small talk.

"It went okay. It turns out her lawyer and I went to undergrad together."

"So, what do they want?"

"I don't know an amount, but he said they want to be fair. He said his client doesn't want anything for herself, just something for the child."

"Well," Obitz said, "unless they have something in writing from Russell, neither she nor the child is entitled to anything."

What Obitz said was accurate. Clearly the claimant and Russell hadn't been a couple long enough for her to qualify as his partner under common law. And, even if DNA testing determined Russell to be the father, it was meaningless unless he had made a commitment in writing.

"So, you don't know if they have anything in writing?" Obitz asked.

"No, not yet. But I'm going to press them on that point because theirs is the only claim I've got."

"That's encouraging," Obitz said. "Given all the news coverage about Russell's murder and, before that, him getting a bunch of money for selling the business, I'm surprised you haven't heard from some long-lost relative or Godchild."

Wilson didn't respond. He had a responsibility to Russell. He had to defend Russell's estate against bogus claims. But he found himself hoping he could allow a reasonable portion to go to Russell's child. Even if Russell had refused responsibility, Wilson hoped something could be worked out.

"Michael, can you tell me anything more about your interest in the estate?" He had asked Obitz the same question in their initial conversation.

"No. I'm sorry. But I hope to very soon."

"Good, because the train is moving down the tracks and the government will end up getting most everything."

"I'll be in touch, Sherman. Stay well."

Hanging up, Sherman Wilson thought: Obitz has something and it's in writing. I don't care how important he is, how successful he is, I'm not answering any more of his questions until he shows his hand.

He also needed some answers from A. J. Washington, Julia Jamison's lawyer.

Washington answered the phone himself. "Sherm, good to hear from you."

"I need answers to a couple of things, A. J." Wilson decided the time had come for directness.

"Fire away."

"Do you have documentation of any kind?"

"Yes. They exchanged a lot of emails."

"But did Kincaid make any promise to be supportive of your client or the child?"

"I'm going to hold off answering that one till I know where you're headed."

"Well, it's a tell-me-now or tell-me-later kind of thing," Wilson countered. "Do you have physical evidence?"

"Yes, as I said previously. Yes."

"It better be DNA."

"It is."

"A. J., you know as well as I do that you don't have a legal claim unless Russell committed it to paper and signed the damn thing. I sympathize with your client, but no court will. I'm moving ahead with the estate, so you need to provide whatever you have pronto. Agreed?"

"I'll get back to you."

Wilson got up from his desk, put on his jacket and walked outside. He did his best thinking while walking. Rain or shine, hot or cold, it didn't matter. Walking cleared his head of extraneous stuff and, time after time, produced answers.

He'd been leaning in this direction. Now he was sure. He'd try to find a way to allow a small part of the estate to go to the benefit of Russell's kid.

The missing piece to the whole puzzle was what Obitz was up to. But time was on his side. Obitz would have to step forward soon.

CHAPTER 48

Michael Obitz knew the clock was ticking but he also knew he had a winning hand.

He phoned Florence Treadwell. "Florence, it's time we talk confidentially to someone in Waterford about Russell's estate and his father's wishes. Who should that be?"

Without hesitation, Florence said, "Steve Insley. He's our mayor and he's as solid as a rock."

"Okay. Will you, please, contact the mayor and see if you and he can be in my office tomorrow afternoon at, let's say, three."

"I will. Can I tell him it's concerning the Kincaid estate?"

"Yes, but nothing more, and only if you're sure he won't breathe a word to anyone."

"I'm sure he won't. I'll phone your office to confirm the appointment."

A smile spread across Florence's face as she punched in Steve Insley's number.

She told Insley what Obitz had said she could say. He didn't press for more, promised he wouldn't say anything to anyone, and said he would pick her up at two.

+++

Michael Obitz greeted Steve Insley as if he was the most important person for states around. That was his style, developed while in politics and polished to perfection as a lawyer.

"Mr. Mayor, I cannot absolutely guarantee what I am about to say will come to pass because we have a couple relatively minor things to pin down ..."

Insley was in the dark, wondering what this prominent West Virginian was going to reveal.

" ... but your town stands to get a substantial amount of money."

Eyebrows raised, Insley leaned forward.

Obitz passed a single sheet of paper to Insley. It was the handwritten cover note Junior Kincaid wrote to Florence Treadwell.

"I'll give you a minute to read it."

Insley read it carefully, re-reading the sentence that said if Russell died after selling the company the remaining proceeds "shall pass on to the Town of Waterford, to be used as its citizens decide."

He was silent for a moment. "Does this mean what I think it means?"

"Yes," Obitz replied, looking first at Insley and then at Florence, who was smiling broadly.

"Oh, my goodness," Insley said. "I can't believe this. Oh ... you said there are some few things to pin down."

"Yes, but we are all but certain Russell died without a will or trust. We've been in touch with his lawyer, who has confirmed that. To date, we have only one claim against Russell's estate and I believe it is invalid. Those couple of things need to be buttoned up but I do not see a problem."

Insley looked over at Florence and matched his smile with hers.

"You haven't asked about the money. Russell received eighty-five million. We need to do some research regarding taxes but I believe you can count on receiving something like seventy million net."

"Oh, my goodness," Insley repeated. "Miss Florence, can you imagine what this will mean to Waterford?"

"You folks have had a tough time of it lately," Obitz said. "It's your call, but my advice is that you get together with your Town Council in executive session and agree on a proposal or proposals to present to the town. Can you trust your Town Council members to keep this confidential?"

"I feel sure I can, once I explain what is at stake."

"It's important you know who else knows about the existence of this letter from Junior Kincaid," Obitz said. "It's you, Florence, your Police Chief Frank Wharton, State Police Superintendent Don Blackford, his Chief Homicide Detective Spencer Atkins, myself and several members of my firm.

"Give me a few days to make sure there are no complications before you talk with your Council members. Meantime, you might be thinking about how you would like the money to be allocated so it best benefits Waterford."

No one else was in the elevator on the ride down from Michael Obitz's office, so Insley, without warning, reached out and gave Florence a hug to remember. "Oh, I can't believe this. I can't."

"I wanted to tell someone," Florence said as they walked to Insley's car, "but I couldn't. Frank knows the content of the letter but I don't think he knows how much money might be involved. The reason Frank knows anything about this is because the State Police wanted him informed as part of the investigation into Russell's murder."

Florence told Insley how she discovered the letter while digging through personnel files. "The only reason I did it was because Frank and the State Police Detective Atkins directed we check the files for terminations and disciplinary actions."

The wheels were turning inside Insley's head as he turned onto the Interstate, headed for Waterford. "I need to give this a lot more thought, but once we know for sure we will be getting the money and how much, I believe I will recommend creating a citizens' committee to work with the Council and, together, to come up with a plan. Then, maybe we have a special election, so everyone feels they've had a say.

"We have urgent needs and longer-term ones, and we need to set priorities. I've been working with the state on marketing the plant; that's been my number one priority. I want to get someone in there who will hire our people and pay them a living wage."

"I hope people appreciate how fortunate we are to have you as mayor," Florence said, patting Insley on his shoulder.

"You're very kind, Florence. We have a tremendous opportunity and challenge ahead of us. And, whether or not we end up having a citizens' committee, you can bet I will be calling on you for help."

Michael Obitz knew the time had come to discuss the specifics of Junior Kincaid's communication with Russell's lawyer, Sherman Wilson. He decided he would drive to Parkersburg rather than have Wilson drive to Charleston.

When Obitz phoned, Wilson offered the opposite but Obitz insisted.

"Straighten up the office a bit," Wilson said to his secretary as soon as he hung up. "We're having an important visitor at two."

Obitz's black Jaguar pulled up in front of Wilson's office at five of the hour.

"Sherman," he belted out, right hand extended. "It's good to meet you in person."

"Likewise, Michael. Thank you for driving up."

"Give me the grand tour, Sherman."

"It won't take long. We have a conference room over there, a small library next to it, a combination copy room/kitchen there, one spare office, and mine."

"So, no partners?" Obitz asked.

"No, sir. Though at times I use an intern."

They went into the conference room and began.

Obitz pulled the original and a copy of Junior Kincaid's cover letter and attachment and passed both across the table.

"These are the originals. I wanted you to see them so you know they are genuine. I also have a copy I will leave for you."

Wilson read Junior Kincaid's hand-written letter, taking longer than Obitz expected. Then he skimmed through the typewritten attachment.

He took his glasses off and placed them on the table. Taking a deep breath, he said, "I met Russell's father only once. What a man he must have been."

Pleased and taken aback by the warmth of Wilson's reaction, Obitz replied. "I knew him very well. He was a fine gentleman. Someone who never forgot how blessed he was. His father and he built a fine business and gave so much back to the community." Obitz restrained himself from saying what he thought about Russell's selfish actions because he knew Wilson and Russell had been friends.

Then Obitz told Wilson he had been working with the police in West Virginia, Ohio, and Waterford, and that they had found no evidence of any documentation or the existence of any potential claimants that might affect Junior Kincaid's directive.

"And, I have only the one claim," Wilson said. "The one in Huntington on behalf of the boy."

"Does that attorney have any document signed by Russell?"

Feeling more at ease now to share what he knew with Obitz, Wilson said, "He referred to emails, which I have not seen. And, he said they have DNA proof that Russell fathered the boy."

"Neither of those will hold up in any court, you know."

"I'm inclined to agree but I want to see the emails before I'm completely comfortable."

Wilson had intended to hold off discussing the next subject until later, but decided to put it on the table now.

"Michael, assuming the DNA is positive, I'd like to suggest that Waterford consider setting aside a modest amount for this boy. I've met with the woman once and her attorney twice and I am convinced they are sincere. And, while I did not know Russell's father well, I would think, based on what you and others have said about him, he would approve of this."

Obitz thought for a minute. He'd been in Wilson's presence for less than a half hour but it had been long enough to form a positive impression. What Wilson just said reinforced that impression. Junior Kincaid most certainly would make sure any son Russell fathered, whether through marriage or not, was cared for.

"I agree," Obitz said, "Junior would do just that. I'll want to meet the mother, and you and I will want to structure any possible payment so it is held in trust for the boy. I cannot speak for Waterford but I will recommend it consider such a payment. We can discuss an amount in the days ahead. Sound good?"

Just as Obitz had formed an impression of Wilson, Wilson found he liked and trusted Obitz. This prominent attorney had gone out of his way to treat Wilson as an equal, starting with the insistence of driving the seventy-five or so miles to Parkersburg.

"I look forward to working with you, Sherman."

"The feeling is mutual, Michael."

CHAPTER 49

Phil had encouraging news for Ella Mae and Wally.

"I've got an interview tomorrow."

"Fantastic, Philly Boy, where?" Wally asked.

"In Parkersburg ... with a recycling company. It takes aluminum cans, cleans them, melts them down and casts them into fifty-pound ingots."

Phil, Wally and Ella Mae had worked in the casting department at Kincaid for years until they didn't.

"So, you might be doing kind of the same stuff you did before?" Ella Mae asked.

"Maybe. If ... if I get the job," Phil responded. "This is just an interview."

"God love you," Ella Mae said. "They damn-well better hire you or we'll come picket them."

Ella Mae had her rough edges, but no one could have a better, more supportive friend. She loved Wally and, early on, had "adopted" Phil as her at-work son.

"Are they looking to hire more than just one person?" Wally asked.

"I don't know. I'll try to find out. Wish me luck."

"You've got that," Wally said.

Darlene came over to the table. "Why are you three so happy? Someone hit the Super Lotto?"

"No, I'm never gonna win that damn thing," Ella Mae responded.

"For starters, you gotta buy a damn ticket," Darlene said.

"Oh, shit, maybe that's why I haven't won," Ella Mae shot back.

"Philly Boy's got a job interview," Wally said.

"Well, hooray for you, Philly Boy. Breakfast's on the house — for you. Not for you two," Darlene said, looking first at Wally and then at Ella Mae, who gave her the finger.

Dagwood overheard the good news and, wanting to be a part of the celebration, screeched out, "Philly Boy, Philly Boy."

Darlene shook her head as she so often did when Dagwood improvised. "Scoot over. Tell me all about it."

Phil repeated for Darlene what he'd told Ella Mae and Wally, emphasizing that, so far, it was only an interview.

Wally then changed the subject. "What's the latest on our favorite murder mystery?"

Darlene replied that not much seemed to be happening. "Jake and Miss Florence got their phones and computers back. Jake's hired a lawyer. Frank's no longer meeting every day with that state cop, Atkins. I'm thinking this may turn out to be one of those cold cases."

"That wouldn't hurt my feelings," Wally said.

"Mine either," Ella Mae said. "That'd be friggin' fantastic."

"What about the theory that Allied had Russell popped?" Phil asked.

"I don't hear much of anything about that," Darlene responded. "I still think it makes a lot of sense. Jake was the one who came up with that idea. I sure don't put it past those people at Allied. Just look at what they did to our little town."

CHAPTER 50

Cleveland P.D. Detective Roscoe Barnes had not come up with anything linking anyone at Allied Manufacturing to Russell Kincaid's murder.

While not every top manager at Allied had a squeaky-clean reputation, there was nothing suspicious about any of them. In fact, what Allied was paying Russell was a relative pittance. And, by limiting his consulting agreement to two years, he'd be out of the picture totally in no time at all. Those factors, plus the fact they had not felt obliged to make Russell a corporate officer, combined to argue against an Allied-orchestrated hit.

Barnes had reported all of this back to his West Virginia counterpart, Detective Spence Atkins.

"I'm finding nothing," he said. "I've returned Elise Fortney's phone and computer to her. Nothing of any importance on either. We've kept Russell Kincaid's computer, but there's nothing helpful on it either. Anything new at your end?"

"No," Spence said. "Same thing. Nothing showed up on any cell phones or computers here either. We're in a kind-of holding pattern. We've always believed that if this killing was local, we'd need someone to commit a slip-of-the-tongue or brag about it.

"Frank Wharton, the local Chief, has his ear to the ground. He's a good man, a good cop. People trust him. If there's anything to be heard, Frank will hear it."

Spence then told Barnes he was working on a couple of new homicides in the state. "I'm trying to solve those suckers while they're fresh. I'll stay on the Waterford case, but I'm counting on Frank to advise me if he learns of anything."

"We can't win them all," Barnes said.

"That's what I've told Frank," Spence said. "All we can do is do our best. One good thing about the Waterford case is it sure looks like a one-and-done type of murder. This was someone on a single-purpose mission, not someone who's a threat to others."

"I agree," Barnes said. "Keep me informed and I'll do the same."

Proper legal notice of Russell Kincaid's death having been published and adequate time having passed, Sherman Wilson was closing in on finalizing the estate. He now had a compilation of Russell's debts and had been able to segregate the amount of wealth attributable to the business sale from the amount of personal wealth unrelated to the transaction.

Michael Obitz's team of lawyers had not found anything of substance in West Virginia or Ohio that would interfere with implementing the wishes of Russell's father that Waterford benefit. The one loose end was what to do about Julia Jamison's claim.

Wilson set up another meeting with A. J. Washington, Julia Jamison's attorney. He told Washington in advance that he needed to see the DNA documentation and the emails the lawyer had said existed. Time was of the essence, he said, because he was about to complete his work on the estate.

Washington knew that even with what he had, his claim most likely would not prevail in a court of law. He was counting on Wilson agreeing to "do the right thing" in memory of the deceased client. Washington did not know the City of Waterford had any involvement in the outcome.

"Here is what we have," Washington said, handing a folder across his desk to Wilson. "An analysis comparing Russell Kincaid's DNA with the boy's. It's a match, as you can see."

Although not familiar with this type of printout, Wilson could see what appeared to be tracking. Also, there was a brief written and signed finding at the bottom that confirmed the match.

The emails Washington had referenced were exchanges between Russell and Julia Jamison. They ranged from him saying what great sex they were having, to how much he loved her, to agreeing they should make plans to marry. Then the tone changed to she should have been on the pill, I'm married, get the abortion, and "come on, baby, take the damn money."

"Clearly," Washington said, "your client knew damn well he impregnated my client. You don't see him accusing anyone else."

Wilson hadn't arrived at the meeting doubting Russell was the father. Now he knew for certain.

"A. J., I need to know the amount you want considered. I will neither accept nor reject whatever amount you provide today. What I will do is consider it and get back to you. I remind you that your claim doesn't have a chance of prevailing in court should you seek that remedy."

Washington paused for a few seconds, as if he needed to come up with a figure he had not already developed.

Then he said, "My client is a proud woman, a proud woman who is committing her life to raising their son. She is not wanting anything for herself, only for the boy."

Wilson waited patiently for the dollar figure.

"She is determined his educational needs be met."

"A. J., give me a figure," Wilson said, a hint of a smile showing.

"Two million."

Wilson purposely showed no reaction to the amount but said, "If we agree to do something, I believe there needs to be a trust with, say, you, Ms. Jamison, and a third person as trustees until the boy reaches maturity."

"We would agree to that," Washington replied.

"I'll get back to you."

Wilson was anxious to brief Michael Obitz on his meeting with Washington, which he did in a brief phone conversation.

"What do you think about the two million?" he asked Obitz.

"I think it's a bit high. But, of course, it's not our decision to make — it will be Waterford's."

"Yes," Wilson said, "but a recommendation from you will carry great weight." Wilson knew he was appealing to Obitz's ego; he also knew that a recommendation from a person of Obitz's stature and persuasive skill could carry the day.

Wilson reminded Obitz he had said he wanted to meet Ms. Jamison.

" Maybe," Obitz said, "but you've met her and you came away somewhat impressed, isn't that right?"

"Yes. But I still think you should meet her before we decide on an amount to seek from Waterford." Again, Wilson wanted to make sure he had Obitz fully committed to the plan.

"Okay, set it up. We'll go see her together."

Wilson didn't reveal to A. J. Washington who he was bringing to the meeting, just that the person would have a say as to what if anything might be offered to Julia Jamison.

Any lawyer in West Virginia would recognize Michael Obitz, and when he introduced himself to Washington it had the desired effect.

Washington thought, but didn't say, Jeez, what am I up against?

Then Obitz, looking away from Washington and Wilson, turned to Julia Jamison, and in his softest, most gentle tone said, "Ms. Jamison, tell me about your son."

Initially a bit tense, she immediately and noticeably relaxed. She proceeded to say how much she loved him, how proud she was of him, how smart and handsome he was. Then she pulled out a couple of photos, which Obitz inspected and passed on to Wilson.

"He's a fine looking boy, Ms. Jamison. And he's very fortunate to have you as his mother."

Wilson knew Obitz was hooked. He was sure Obitz would move heaven and earth to see that the youngster was taken care of.

The conversation then turned to the subject of a trust. Both Obitz and Wilson were careful not to promise anything, but the mere fact this meeting had taken place, coupled with the positive chemistry between Obitz and Julia Jamison, left A. J. Washington encouraged, even confident.

CHAPTER 51

The next stop for Michael Obitz and Sherman Wilson would be a closed, informal meeting with Steve Insley and the other four members of the Waterford Town Council.

The decision was made to hold the meeting in Obitz's offices in Charleston.

Insley had, at Obitz's suggestion, confidentially briefed each of the four on the nature of the meeting, but not until the morning of the meeting. He had read to them the pertinent paragraphs of Junior Kincaid's hand-written directive.

Jaws dropped. All four were as unbelieving as Insley had been when he first learned of the intended bequest.

Then, immediately following that brief meeting, they boarded a van and headed to Charleston for their meeting with Obitz. As directed, nothing was said about the subject on the drive to Obitz's office, lest the driver leak to someone. And, they remained quiet on the 18-floor elevator ride.

Obitz and Wilson walked into the conference room together and Obitz began immediately after the introductions.

"As you all know, Junior Kincaid had an abiding love for your town. It was his home; it had been his parents' home. He hoped his company would continue to be family-owned and continue in Waterford long after his death. But, as you now know from Mayor Insley, he directed that if Russell sold the company, then died with no direct heir, whatever portion of the proceeds from the sale remained, would go to Waterford, to be used as its citizens wished."

No one interrupted. They listened carefully, still in a state of blissful disbelief.

"Sherman, as some of you may know, was Russell's attorney. He has been hard at work since Russell's death to determine if there are any competing claimants. My office has assisted in that effort."

Ever the masterful performer, Obitz walked slowly back and forth at one end of the room as he spoke, looking first at one of the Council members, then another, then another.

"We expect the gift to the town will be on the order of seventy million dollars."

He paused, slowly scanning his audience.

"Each of the five turned, looking first at whoever was seated on either side. Eyes widened and smiles broke out.

"My God," was the prevailing initial response.

Obitz paused for a moment to let what he had just said sink in.

"Ladies and gentlemen, we do have one claim which Sherman and I recommend you consider. From a pure legal standpoint, we agree the claim, in all likelihood, would be rejected by the court. But, let me explain.

"The claimant is a young woman with whom Russell fathered a child. The little boy is going on four now. Russell took no responsibility. In fact, he tried to convince the mother to abort. He made no legal provision for the boy, but there is absolutely no question he is the father. We've seen the evidence. Sherman and I have met the mother. She is very devoted to her son. She is asking nothing for herself, only something for her son — Russell's son. Knowing Junior Kincaid as I did for more than twenty-five years, I believe he would want to make sure this boy, his grandson, was cared for — whether or not he was born out of wedlock.

"So," Obitz said, looking at Wilson, "Sherman and I are in agreement in recommending you consider what you deem to be a fair amount."

Steve Insley spoke up. "Has the mother said what she wants for her son?"

Obitz looked at Wilson. "Sherman, will you please address that?"

"The mother is asking for two million dollars."

No one spoke initially. Insley then asked if that was a firm proposal.

Wilson responded, "That is her request. The amount, if any, is yours to determine."

"What would you recommend?" Insley asked.

Wilson looked at Obitz, who nodded back that Wilson should respond. "I believe the request is fair. I did not know Junior Kincaid well but I agree with Michael that he would want his grandson to be well cared for. I should also say that, without committing you to anything, we did get agreement that if any funds were provided, they would go into a trust to be administered by several people. That would ensure the amount is protected and used as intended."

"I'm a little embarrassed to ask since we just learned the town is getting such a large amount," Insley said, "but would the mother be satisfied with a smaller amount? That's a lot of money."

Obitz responded, "I believe so. Again, the decision is yours to make. But, knowing Junior Kincaid as I did and as, I'm sure, some, if not all, of you did, I believe either that amount or something close to it would honor his memory."

Confident he and Wilson had made their case, Obitz said, "If there are no more questions, I ask you to keep what we discussed today confidential. We want to make absolutely certain we have covered every base. Having some experience myself in politics and government, the last thing you want is to say something and then have to pull it back. I will get back to Steve when all is clear."

"We are sworn to confidentiality," Insley assured. "We will discuss this among ourselves but absolutely no further than that until we hear back from you, Michael."

At this point, Obitz pressed a button at his end of the conference table, the door opened, and two servers entered with a couple of bottles of champagne.

CHAPTER 52

Mayor Steve Insley was still in shock over the amount of money that, it now seemed certain, was coming to Waterford. But he also was feeling the heavy weight of responsibility that had been placed on him and the Town Council members to administer this newfound wealth wisely.

Two days after their meeting with Obitz and Wilson, Insley and the other four Council members met at Insley's house. They brainstormed ideas about how the funds might be used — everything from buying the Kincaid plant, to replacing the worn out gym at the middle school, improving the park at Wilkens Ferry Landing, and making cash payments to each adult resident.

They were clear on one thing. They would seek input from their fellow residents and then put forward a package to be voted on.

Working until a few minutes before midnight, they agreed they needed to communicate to the people of Waterford as soon as possible. The town needed a boost. Both exhausted and exhilarated, they agreed to meet again at Insley's house in two days. Meantime, Insley asked them to refine their thoughts.

Insley received a call from Obitz confirming there were no claimants other than Ms. Jamison, so he could go ahead, when ready, with communicating the news to the town. He told Obitz he and the Council members had met once and would meet again that night. Then he took Obitz through some of the suggestions on which they would seek input from the townspeople.

Obitz agreed with the approach and then raised the Jamison issue.

"We didn't discuss it at our initial meeting but will tonight," Insley said, without committing to an amount. "I hope we can reach agreement on it tonight and, if we do, I will phone your office in the morning so either Mr. Wilson or you can decide when and who advises her attorney."

The members of the Town Council arrived at Insley's house at six in the evening. As he hoped would be the case, each of them had given additional thought to priorities for use of the funds.

"Before we get into your ideas," Insley began, "I'd like to know your thinking on an amount for Russell's child."

All agreed a contribution should be made. Two favored offering one million, one favored the full two million, and one abstained. Insley offered one and a half million. All five then agreed on Insley's figure. Insley said he would advise Obitz the next day.

After considerable back and forth, they agreed to have a highly publicized town hall meeting at the middle school that would be simultaneously broadcast on Waterford's lone radio station. The Council would offer an initial list of projects to be considered, but make clear it wanted people to suggest their own priorities for the common good. They agreed to set a deadline for receiving suggestions. Then they would compile the responses and assemble a list of the top five. This would be an initial phase, accounting for only a modest portion of the total funds available. The package of five choices would then be put to a community-wide vote.

They wanted this initial spending commitment to be both uplifting and prudent. There would be plenty of time in the coming months and years to develop and fund other priorities.

"I suggest we announce at our regularly scheduled Council meeting next week that we will have a major announcement to make the following week," Insley said. "We'll want to make sure the middle school gym is available. Also, our radio station needs to be alerted to cover the event. Meantime, let's be absolutely certain we don't leak. I want to be sure we are the ones who break this news. We don't want to be in a position of chasing rumors or inaccurate reports. This is a fantastic opportunity for our community, and we need to get it right."

The remainder of the meeting was spent exchanging ideas and developing a list of projects.

As planned, Insley phoned Michael Obitz the next morning.

"Steve, how are you?"

"I'm well, Michael, and you."

"Far better than a man my age has a right to expect."

Having learned that Obitz wasn't much for small talk, Insley got right to the point. "Michael, the Council and I agreed you or Mr. Wilson should advise Ms. Jamison's attorney we will contribute one and a half million dollars into a trust for the benefit of her son. We also ask that this decision be kept confidential until we are able to communicate a complete package of information to our townspeople."

He waited for a few seconds, concerned that Obitz might be disappointed with the less-than-full amount.

"I think that is wonderful, Steve. I'll contact Sherman and we'll decide who contacts Ms. Jamison's attorney. I believe it's a very generous amount and reflects very positively on you, the Council members and the benefactor, Junior Kincaid."

Insley was relieved. One item checked off, he thought.

Michael Obitz and Sherman Wilson decided Obitz should make the call to Julia Jamison's lawyer, A. J. Washington.

"It will carry more weight coming from you," Wilson said. "A. J. might be tempted to negotiate with me. I don't think he will with you." Wilson knew he was feeding Obitz's ego a bit but he also believed what he was saying.

"If you say so, Sherman. I'll try to reach Washington as soon as we hang up."

As usual, Washington answered his own phone. Obitz reminded him his client had no valid legal claim. However, he said, the Town Council decided to act as it believed Junior Kincaid, Russell's father, would want it to. And, so, he said, "They will contribute one and a half million dollars into a trust fund for Ms. Jamison's son."

There was no response for five or so seconds.

"Mr. Washington?"

"Yes, Mr. Obitz, I'm here. We accept. I will advise my client, and I know she will appreciate the Council's action and Sherman's and your help."

"A couple of other things, Mr. Washington. It is important that you and Ms. Jamison keep this confidential until Sherman or I advise otherwise. The Waterford Town Council will be hosting a town hall meeting to inform the community of the overall bequest and to seek input on how initial segments might be allocated."

"Absolutely," Washington replied.

"And, second," Obitz said, "we ask that you review with Sherman or me a draft of the trust so we are able to provide input, if desired. My suggestion is to have three trustees: Ms. Jamison, you, and Sherman, assuming he is willing to serve."

"That sounds reasonable, Mr. Obitz. Shall I get back to you or Sherman to confirm?"

"Either is fine."

CHAPTER 53

Rumors were running wild now that the town hall meeting had been scheduled. What could the important announcement be? Was a new company coming to town? Had the Kincaid plant been sold? There had been talk in past years about a Walmart or maybe an Amazon warehouse. Maybe some part of the Federal government. Martinsburg, over in the state's eastern panhandle, had a major Internal Revenue Service facility as well as a Coast Guard operation. Maybe something like that.

So far, Mayor Insley and the Town Council members had maintained their pledge of confidentiality. Frank Wharton, who knew about the windfall from the initial meeting in Michael Obitz's office, wasn't talking. Neither was Florence Treadwell. The fact that something this big could be kept a secret in Waterford was amazing.

No one was more frustrated than Darlene. She was accustomed to being the trusted source of all that was important and some that wasn't. She treasured that role. But, at least for now, her sources had dried up. No one with any authority or knowledge was talking.

Business was better than usual at Darlene's because folks wanted to know what others had heard. Everyone assumed the announcement would be positive. Even the gloomiest were hard-pressed to come up with anything bad.

Having heard so much "big news" conversation as people entered and left the diner, Dagwood, adapting to the moment, would squawk, "Big news, big news" whenever the spirit moved him.

Ella Mae, Wally, and Phil had maintained their three-days-a-week breakfast date.

"What do you think?" Ella Mae asked as they drank their coffee.

"I think somebody's buying the plant." Wally said.

Phil, acting a bit preoccupied, said, "I haven't a clue."

"Oh," Wally said, "I almost forgot. How'd your interview go?"

"Okay, I guess," Phil answered, "but they told me they had a lot of people to interview."

"What do you mean, 'okay, I guess', Philly Boy," Ella Mae jumped in. "Didn't you tell 'em you're the smartest, hardest-working, most skilled s.o.b. in all of West-By-God-Virginia?"

Phil smiled but didn't respond.

Anyone else from Kincaid applying?" Ella Mae asked.

"Not that I know of."

"Did you talk about pay?" Wally asked.

"Yeah. It would be a couple of bucks an hour less than I was getting at the plant, but I'd take it."

"Well, good luck, Philly Boy," Ella Mae said. "If they know what's good for them they'll hire your ass."

"Thanks for the vote of confidence, beautiful lady."

Ella Mae loved "that boy" and she didn't mind at all being called beautiful and a lady.

They returned to speculating about the upcoming announcement.

Busy as things were, Darlene, as usual, found time to come to their table.

"Okay," Wally said, "What's your prediction?"

Never before at a loss for words, Darlene replied, "I have no damn idea. Dagwood knows as much as I do ... maybe more. Ask him."

"I did," Wally said. "All he said is 'big news, big news'."

"What about all your 'reliable sources'?" Ella Mae asked.

"They're not saying a damn thing. I'm gonna remember this; I'm making a list. I might raise the price I charge them or burn their damn toast or something. You know me, I don't get mad. I get even."

Wally, who should have known from experience not to take a drink of his coffee while Darlene was talking, choked and sputtered for what seemed like a full minute while Ella Mae, Phil, and Darlene watched and laughed.

CHAPTER 54

An unusually mild winter had morphed into a wet but welcome spring. Frank Wharton hadn't been to either Darlene's or the Roadside Bar for some time. Curious to learn what they might be hearing, he decided to visit Augie first, then Darlene.

Remembering that late morning was the best time to catch Augie, he drove the short distance to the bar. He arrived a half hour before opening. Augie was in the back, putting the final touches on a cursory cleaning of the men's room.

"Chief, haven't seen you in a while. Anything happening?"

"Still investigating," Frank replied. "Anybody here bragging about killing Russell?"

"Nope. The same old speculation. Most seem to think Jake Walter did it. But, if he did, they hope he gets away with it.

"What's the big announcement?" Augie asked.

"You need to come to the gym or turn your radio on."

"I figure you know what it's all about," Augie said, smiling.

"Stay tuned, Augie," Frank said with a straight face.

Frank returned to his office and worked on his department's budget proposal for the coming fiscal year. He had feared losing one position, maybe two because the town's budget had been battered by the Kincaid plant closing. He had worked and re-worked the numbers and, if he had to, he was going to ask if his officers were willing to share in a pay cut in order to save the positions. Now, with the incredibly good news on its way, he hoped he would be able to keep the department at its present level.

By now, it was two thirty, so he'd head over to Darlene's.

Dagwood offered up his usual "Hi, Darlin'."

"Hi, Dagwood, what's new, buddy?"

That was all the encouragement Dagwood needed. "Big news, big news," he responded cheerily.

Darlene followed Frank to a booth toward the rear. She figured he might know what the announcement was but held off asking.

"What's new with you, Hon?"

"Not much. How about you? What are you hearing?"

"About Russell or about the announcement?"

"Both. Russell, first."

"Honestly, nothing new. I still think Allied had it done. That makes sense to me. You know a lot more than I do."

"That's part of the investigation," Frank said. "The Cleveland P.D. is working closely with Detective Atkins in Charleston. They keep me informed and I keep my ear to the ground here.

"You're not hearing anyone saying they know who did it or bragging that they did?"

"No. I'm not picking up anything. I hear a few still saying they think Jake must have done it. But they don't know. They're just yakking."

Darlene had waited as long as she could.

"What's the big announcement, Frank?"

Frank chuckled.

"You know, damn it, you know," Darlene said.

Frank just shook his head.

"Okay, Mister, if I find out you've leaked to someone else, I'll personally flatten your damn tires," she threatened with a smile.

"If you do, you'll earn an overnight stay in one of our lovely holding cells," Frank responded.

"Enjoy your lunch. I haven't spiked it with anything that'll do permanent damage. But you might want to stay close to the john for a day or two."

Frank laughed as Darlene headed off to the front of the diner. The salisbury steak, one of his favorites, tasted just fine.

CHAPTER 55

Mayor Insley and the Town Council members met two days before the town hall to finalize their recommendations for funding. They would make clear that, with the exception of the commitment already made to Julia Jamison, these were their suggestions and that suggestions from the community would be given equal weight.

The first recommendation was to begin negotiations to buy the plant from Allied with the help of a partial grant from the state. Assuming this recommendation was ultimately approved, the Town Council would decide whether to pay cash or finance a portion of the purchase. Insley was betting he could convince Allied to drop its price to as low as one and a half million. If he succeeded in getting the three hundred thousand grant from the state, Waterford's share would be one million, two hundred thousand.

This particular recommendation was near and dear to Insley's heart because he believed, if properly marketed and developed, the plant was a solid investment — one that would provide jobs and help Waterford control its own destiny.

The second was a three thousand dollar cash gift to each adult town resident. Given that there were approximately two thousand adult residents, that outlay would be about six million dollars. Insley and the Town Council members had gone back and forth on this one but finally agreed it would have a positive, morale-boosting effect.

The third was a new gym and multi-purpose room for the middle school. They quickly agreed on this one.

The fourth and final one they would propose was to build a picnic shelter, basketball/volleyball court, snack bar, and new rest rooms at the park at Wilkens Ferry Landing and name it "The Jeffrey Kincaid Memorial Park."

All told, and assuming they paid all cash for the plant, these recommendations might account for eight or nine million dollars of the seventy-or-so million the city would be receiving. The commitment of one and a half million dollars to the Jamison boy would take the total to about ten million.

Insley was prepared to advocate for each but, again, to invite input and specific suggestions from the community. Each resident would be mailed a form which detailed the four recommendations, asked for a "yes" or "no" vote, and added a page for individual suggestions.

CHAPTER 56

The town hall was set to start at six, but the gym was packed by five-thirty. In anticipation of an overflow crowd, a large screen and speakers had been set up in the school's central courtyard. And, Waterford's very own, privately owned and operated radio station was on site to reach those who were not in attendance.

Mayor Insley and the Town Council members were seated on the stage. Following the Pledge of Allegiance, Insley spoke.

He began by thanking everyone for coming and then moved directly to the subject.

"We've been going through some very tough times lately, but we are a town that sticks together. We care about each other. We help each other."

Darlene, sitting in the front row with Ella Mae, Wally and Phil, whispered to Ella Mae, "Get to the damn point, Steve."

"This evening," Insley continued, I have some very good news to share. You all know how much Jeffrey Kincaid and Junior Kincaid loved our town."

"Jeez," Darlene whispered again, "I'm gonna wet my little thong ..."

Ella Mae covered her mouth with both hands and somehow resisted laughing out loud.

"Even though Kincaid Fabricators as a business is no longer here in town," Insley continued, "the spirit and love of these two wonderful men is very much with us.

"This evening, I am pleased to announce a major gift from Junior Kincaid to our city to be used as you, the citizens, desire."

"What? How much?" This time, Darlene's voice was more than a whisper.

"Was that you, Darlene?" Insley asked, displaying a huge grin.

"Yes, it was," she replied not at all shyly.

"Okay," he said, "the gift is in the neighborhood of seventy million dollars."

Even Darlene was quiet for a moment as the figure of seventy million was absorbed. Then she was the first to jump up, throw her arms in the air and squeal. Others joined in with shouts and applause.

Inside and outside the gym, people jumped up and down, hugged each other, fist-bumped and high-fived.

Insley let the celebration go on without interruption for a couple of minutes. Then he projected the first of several Power Point slides that set forth the Town Council's initial recommendations, stressing that residents would, as he put it, "be the deciders."

All four of the recommendations attracted applause. The second, the one that proposed a gift of three thousand dollars to each adult resident, got the loudest and most sustained response.

Insley then explained the commitment already made to Russell Kincaid's child. Most in the community figured he had two or three or four children somewhere out there because of his well-known philandering. They were surprised the number was only one.

The mayor had been concerned some would object to the size of the grant to the boy's trust fund but, after he explained that "Junior Kincaid most certainly would provide for his grandson if he were alive today," any potential questioning evaporated.

Next, Insley explained the procedure for submitting ideas and voting on specific recommendations. He sensed that people were only half-listening because the excitement level was so high.

The time reserved for questions was only partially used. People wanted to talk to their neighbors or whomever was seated or standing next to them.

Waterford had come alive. For many, the fact their jobs at Kincaid had been eliminated was temporarily displaced by the exciting news of the night.

The gym didn't empty out until almost nine. No one was in a hurry to go home; no one wanted the evening to end. The conversations centered on the proposals Insley had described but also expanded to other possible projects. Things like new street lights on Cedar Street, a sprucing up of downtown, and the aggressive marketing of Waterford as a great place to work, play and live.

Darlene had closed the diner at four so she and her staff could attend the town hall. She usually stayed open until nine. While at the event, she had passed the word to Frank Wharton, Florence Treadwell, and the trio of

Ella Mae, Wally and Phil to come in the diner's back door afterwards for coffee and pie a la mode.

Dagwood's cage hadn't yet been covered for the night so, even though the group didn't enter through the front door, he could hear them in the back and called out his familiar greeting repeatedly, mixing in an occasional "big news, big news".

No one thought to press either Frank or Florence on whether they knew anything about the night's announcement in advance. Neither said much; they sat back, enjoying the happiness that surrounded them and the fresh peach pie topped with vanilla ice cream.

To no one's surprise, Darlene and Ella Mae were the most vocal.

"That Junior Kincaid," Darlene said. "What a sweetheart of a man. To do what he did ... is that unbelievable or what?"

"I know what I'm doing in the morning right after breakfast with these two clowns," Ella Mae said, pointing at Wally and Phil, "I'm driving out to where Junior's buried and putting some flowers on his grave."

True to form, Wally was the first to finish his dessert. "I don't remember all the detail Mayor Steve took us through, but all four of those recommendations seem sensible to me."

"Especially the three thousand you'd get," Ella Mae said.

"Yeah, sure, that'll be nice. But I really like the idea of the town owning the plant. That way we all have a say about what goes in there. It'll be like we are shareholders. You know what I mean? We'll feel like family again."

That hit home with Miss Florence. "I agree, Wally, and that's what Junior would want." Florence pulled a Kleenex from her purse and dabbed a tear, at which point Frank reached over and gave her a hug.

They talked for more than an hour before Darlene issued her good-natured ultimatum. "Okay, I've got to be here at five in the morning so I can feed some of you beautiful people at six. So, get the hell out of here."

"Not before saying good night to Dagwood," Ella Mae said. So they all stumbled into the partially lit dining area to bid a good evening to the town's favorite (and only) African Grey Parrot. Dagwood reciprocated with repeated "Bye darlin's" even after Darlene covered his cage for the night.

Walking to their cars, Frank took Florence's hand. "I'm so happy for the town," he said.

"So am I, Frank. So am I."

CHAPTER 57

The mood had changed overnight in Waterford. Fewer people were talking about needing to move; more were saying they'd hunker down, spend the promised cash prudently, pick up odd jobs whenever and wherever they could, plant a bigger garden, and hope someone would move into the plant and hire locally.

The Charleston and Parkersburg television stations and newspapers had covered the town hall meeting, interviewing the mayor, Council members and ecstatic attendees, and accurately reporting the key parts of the announcement. Two major networks picked up the story and aired it across the country as a "good news" feature.

This kind of exposure was priceless. Insley and his Council members already were thinking of ways they could build on it. Ground breaking on the gym, the park, massive cleanup and construction in the plant, those kinds of things. Get the Governor, the Congressman, maybe even one or both of the Senators out here; photo ops galore.

Frank Wharton hadn't felt this good for months. For too long, the stress had been awful. Now, it was like a two hundred pound boulder had been lifted off his chest. The town he loved, the people he loved — and, with very few exceptions, who loved him back — were once again their optimistic selves.

Small-town folks, maybe particularly those in West Virginia, tend to be wavers. The wave can be a hand out a car window or just a couple or three or four fingers raised off the steering wheel. Knowing the other person is irrelevant. Driving around town as he did every day, Frank picked up on this. Damn, everybody's waving again, he thought, a smile spreading across his face.

The mass excitement the night before had prevented him from talking with the mayor, so he walked down the hall to talk with Insley.

"Great speech, Mr. Mayor," he said, as they embraced each other.

"Thanks. It's easy when you have that kind of good news to announce."

They talked about the Council's recommendations. Sure, the grant of three thousand dollars per adult was a winner. That was a given. But Frank agreed that acquiring the plant and succeeding in getting a major tenant or tenants could be a game changer for the long-term.

Insley's mind was moving at warp speed. "The projects we talked about — all of them — require workers. We can fill a bunch of those temporary jobs right here. We've got to make that plant attractive. We can do a lot of that with our own people. And, assuming we get approval for the gym and multi-purpose room and all the improvements at the park, we can write into the contracts a requirement to hire locally."

"Are you confident you can get Allied to lower the price of the plant and get the state to make the grant?" Frank asked. "Or is our hand weakened by them knowing we now have all this money?"

"I'm pretty darned confident about both. Allied doesn't want that building. They know they won't get two million and they have good reason to believe it won't sell fast. So a million and a half cash now is a good deal for them. Regarding the grant, the state is pretty well committed. The people at Economic Development in Charleston want to help projects they are confident will succeed and reflect positively on them. Our resources and our commitment to making this project a success give us an advantage over a lot of projects they consider. This should turn out to be a real showcase for them."

Insley said he was going to phone both Al Donaldson at Allied and Economic Development in Charleston the next day. "By then," he said, "I expect both will have seen or heard about the media coverage."

"Who the hell is taking care of your store these days?" Frank asked, resuming the smile he'd shown most of the morning.

Insley laughed. "I've been so busy with all of this stuff I don't know if I'm making money or going bankrupt."

"Okay, boss," Frank said, "I've got to get back to my office and work on my budget. Should I assume I can keep those two positions we thought we might have to eliminate?"

"The Council will decide," Insley replied, "but, yes, include them in your request."

Walking down the hall, Frank began humming, "Zip a dee doo dah, zip a dee ay," a happy tune he remembered his father singing years before when the two of them went fishing in the Maplethorn. He hadn't thought about that song for years.

CHAPTER 58

Al Donaldson, Allied Manufacturing's president, knew of the Waterford announcements by the time he got the call from Mayor Insley. By chance, he'd seen a segment about the town and its windfall on the Cleveland station he normally watched.

"So, Mr. Mayor," he said before even saying "hello", "you folks are rolling in the dough."

Insley was prepared for this. "It's a start on what you took away from us," he countered good naturedly.

They both laughed.

"So, you're going to buy the plant for two million?" Donaldson asked.

"No, but maybe for one and a half."

"Oh, it's worth more than that."

"Al, you're smart enough to know you're never going to get two million. You also know that, unless Waterford buys it, it will, in all likelihood, sit unsold for a long time while you pay the property taxes and other expenses. And, you sure don't need an Economics 101 tutorial from me on the present value of money. I don't have the town's okay to do a deal yet. But, I expect to get it. And when I do, I'll come at you with a take-it-or-leave-it offer of one and a half million. Just sayin'."

"Steve," Donaldson paused for a couple of seconds and then replied, "you're the kind of guy we like to hire here at Allied. Call me if you ever get tired of selling nuts and bolts at your little store."

They ended the call with Insley certain he had a deal. All he needed was the residents' concurrence.

Business continued to be brisk at Darlene's. To celebrate the news about Junior Kincaid's gift to the town and in deference to Dagwood's newfound favorite words, she added a "Big News" special to the menu every evening. One night it would be chicken fried steak, the next, beef stroganoff, and so forth. Whatever the entree, the price was five ninety-nine.

At breakfast a couple of days after the big announcement, Ella Mae, Wally, and Phil re-hashed what they were hearing.

"I don't have anything to add to what the Mayor proposed," Wally said. "I'm going to vote for all four of them."

A smile on his face, Phil said, "I can sure put that three thousand to good use. I still haven't heard back from my job interview. I did pick up a couple of handyman jobs last week, so my head's still above water."

"The mayor's talking about using some local labor to work on the gym and the park improvements, so get your name on some kind of list for that," Ella Mae suggested.

"I'm wondering if he's already got a prospect in mind for the plant," Wally said.

"If he does, Darlene will know," Ella Mae said. "Darlene! Get over here and talk to your three loveliest customers."

"I can only stay a minute. Every booth has been taken since six thirty. Don't any of these people know how to cook?"

"Don't complain," Ella Mae said, "It sure beats sitting in here with only Dagwood squawking out his "big news" to an empty diner."

"You got that right."

"How are you voting?" Phil asked.

"For all four," Darlene replied. "I may add one of my own — a big, new freezer for the kitchen."

"It's got to be for the common good," Wally said.

Darlene was ready for that. "It is. You're common, Wally, and you, Ella Mae, if you're not common I don't know what is. You eat here. Therefore, common people eating at Darlene's Dream Diner equals the common good. So there."

Wally and Phil laughed. Ella Mae resorted to once again giving Darlene the finger.

"You know what I remember most about the town hall?" Darlene asked and then immediately answered, "seeing how happy Miss Florence was. She loved Junior Kincaid, and the whole family, with the exception of that idiot Russell, loved her. She just glowed, God love her."

Word had leaked out that Junior Kincaid's wishes had been spelled out in a confidential letter to Miss Florence.

"I've been including her in my prayers the last couple nights," Wally said. Ella Mae and Phil nodded agreement. They also agreed they'd vote for all four projects.

"I'm really looking forward to the town owning the plant," Darlene said. "Now we can make sure it doesn't sit out there empty with weeds growing up around it. The mayor believes it can be made into a real showcase for not much money.

"Gotta go," Darlene said, "gotta take care of customers who spend a lot more than you three."

Her hand wrapped around her usual cinnamon roll, Ella Mae opted not to offer her usual "wave" to Darlene.

Steve Insley decided to drive to Charleston to talk with his contacts at Economic Development. He wanted to make sure the three hundred thousand dollar grant was a firm commitment, because he planned to move quickly once the Kincaid monies became available.

After being kidded by the department head at Economic Development about Waterford no longer needing a state grant, Insley reviewed the proposals he had put forward to improve the town. He pledged to work in partnership with ED to market the plant, to work as a good will ambassador and welcoming host.

He stressed the importance of a grant from the state. "The money is important, for sure," he said. "But more important is what it says; it says you believe in the project. That's a positive message to a town that's picking itself up off the ground and to businesses that are looking for a place to expand. A win all the way around."

Insley got the answer he wanted. The money was his if he could get the deal done with Allied.

Driving back to Waterford, his mind was racing. He enjoyed running the hardware store his father had opened nearly forty years earlier. He liked the contact with customers and took pride in being able to meet their specific needs. Waterford folks were willing to pay prices slightly higher than charged at the big box stores in order to support local businesses like his. He appreciated that and he'd stay in the hardware business.

But, being mayor was what really energized him. He was nervous early on in his first year. Now that he was winding up his third year in office, he was comfortable, confident, and clear in what he wanted for his town.

Losing Kincaid Fabricators could have been a fatal blow; more than a few feared it would be. But if he and the Council could get these first four projects done, he was confident Waterford would be on a solid path to recovery.

An early priority would be to clean up the Kincaid plant. The way equipment had been ripped out left a mess of fractured concrete and exposed pipes. He'd keep the costs under control, but it clearly needed some cosmetic refurbishing.

Michael Obitz had checked with Sherman Wilson, Russell's attorney, who told him he expected to be able to release most of the funds to the town in a week or so. Wilson said the initial amount would be about sixty-five million, with another five or ten million to follow in a month or so.

Russell had spent only about two hundred thousand of the eighty-five million he got for selling the business. Wisely, Wilson was holding back a sizeable sum as a cushion for taxes and other expenses.

To be determined was whether the gift would cause Waterford to incur a tax liability. As a city, it was by nature and practical definition, non-profit. Obitz volunteered to make sure no taxes would be owed. If it took special legislation, he knew from experience and extensive contacts how to accomplish that. Everyone, friend or foe, was aware of Obitz's influence.

He and Wilson met again with A. J. Washington and Julia Jamison, this time to talk about the trust that would be established for her son.

At Obitz's urging and with Julia Jamison's approval, Wilson had agreed to be one of the trustees. The other two would be Washington and her.

Then, unprompted, Ms. Jamison said, "I want my son to know this is a gift from his grandfather. And, at the right time, I will make sure he knows that. Raising a child as a single parent isn't easy, but I want him to know that, while his grandfather and father are no longer alive, they are holding our hand."

Washington, Obitz and Wilson looked at each other, in awe of this young woman's wisdom, unselfishness, and love.

Obitz broke the silence. "I said it when we first met, Ms. Jamison, that son of yours is very fortunate to have you as his mother."

She smiled; they all smiled.

CHAPTER 59

State Police Superintendent Don Blackford wanted to be brought current on the homicide investigation. He asked that Spence Atkins, Frank Wharton, and Cleveland P.D. Detective Roscoe Barnes join in a conference call.

The positive economic news about Waterford had put the unsolved Kincaid murder back in the news and Don was feeling some pressure from the Governor's office for not having solved it.

"Spence," he said, "you go first. Where do we stand?"

"Very honestly, we don't have anything definite enough to consider charges against anyone. We've learned a lot about a lot of people, but — so far — it hasn't taken us where we need to be.

"We knew at the beginning that unless we got some kind of break — someone talking, someone bragging or pointing a finger at someone else — this was going to be a tough one. None of those things has happened. They still could, and when and if they do, we'll be ready to rumble."

"So, at this point, who do you consider to be persons of possible interest?"

"Jake Walter, the former plant manager, continues to be a possibility. As we've discussed in the past, he and Kincaid didn't hit it off. We've learned — and we believe he knew — Kincaid wanted him gone even before he sold the company. He's got an attorney now, so we're not talking. Before that, Frank and I talked with him a lot. The anger is very real. But, we don't have anything beyond that. We checked out his phone and computer. Nothing there."

"Who else?" Don asked.

"We considered Beverly Kincaid, Russell's ex. They went through that God-awful divorce several years ago. But she had nothing to gain from his death. She got everything she was going to get in the divorce settlement. She was straight up with us; she didn't feign sorrow. Neither Frank nor I believe she had anything to do with it.

"Then there's Florence Treadwell. Could she have orchestrated it? Possibly. She's super smart, and she was disgusted with Russell's behavior. He unceremoniously demoted her before selling the company. So, there's motive. But there was nothing on her phone or computer, either.

"I talked with the waitress, Monica Salisbury, at The Charleston Club. She and Russell had been having an affair for more than two years and she said they planned to get married. But, as we know, that's what this guy said to a lot of women. She believed him and was genuinely heartbroken by his death. She's not a suspect.

"Frank? Why don't you chime in here. You talked to a couple of people I didn't."

"Yeah. First, I agree with everything Spence just said. I've known Jake Walter for a long time and, even though he had a motive, I just can't see him doing it. He's a good family man with a bunch of life still ahead of him. He's never been in trouble. He's not a hot head by any stretch of the imagination.

"Spence was right on with respect to Beverly Kincaid. She had nothing to gain, everything to lose.

"And, Miss Florence. No way would she be a part of anything like this. Was she upset, damn right. Still is. But orchestrate Russell's murder, no way.

"I talked to a couple of loud-mouthed guys our local bar owner steered me to. But, I'm absolutely sure they were all talk. As you know, no one in town is mourning Russell's death."

"Okay," Don said, "Your turn, Roscoe."

"We've spent a lot of time here in Cleveland looking into whether the leadership at Allied wanted Kincaid out of their hair. It's possible they orchestrated a hit, but I haven't uncovered anything to support that. His employment contract with them was for only two years. They could dump him after that. He was being paid a lot less than their top four or five officers, so there wasn't much of a financial incentive to have him snuffed out.

"I've got some pretty reliable contacts inside a couple of Cleveland crime families and they don't know anything about Kincaid — or Allied, for that matter.

"I talked with Elise Fortney, the woman who worked for Kincaid in Waterford and lived with him here. I don't consider her a suspect. We checked her phone and computer and still have his. We haven't found anything of interest on them.

"Bottom line, so far nothing of use from Cleveland. I've got a lot of other stuff going on in my beloved city. Crime marches on. But I won't forget you guys. I'll stay with it."

"Well, gentlemen," Don said, "I appreciate the update. More than that, I appreciate the weeks, days, and hours you've devoted to this. Frank, I'm sorry we haven't helped you solve this one. It's frustrating for all of us. But, the fact is, we don't solve them all. And, as far as I'm concerned, this isn't a cold case. It's not going to be filed away and forgotten. As long as I'm in this job, it'll remain active.

"Anything else anyone wants to say?"

"Just thanks," Frank said, "to each of you and to anyone who's been working with you. It's an experience I never thought I'd have here in Waterford. I'll stay on it and be in touch if anything comes up."

Don concluded the call by saying he was glad that Waterford is benefiting from the Kincaid estate and that the child he fathered is being taken care of.

Hanging up from the call, Frank took a deep breath before pouring a second mug full of coffee.

CHAPTER 60

All but a few of the questionnaire/ballots had been received and tabulated. All four of the elements Mayor Insley and the Council had recommended drew wide support — especially the individual grants of three thousand dollars and the acquisition of the Kincaid plant.

A fifth proposal, put forward by a number of townspeople, recommended a modest amount of money be designated for "improving the appearance" of downtown Waterford. The Town Council decided to assist each business in this general sprucing up effort. For starters, it would provide and maintain a series of flower boxes stretching the length of the commercial section of Cedar Street.

Town Council had been meeting weekly rather than monthly ever since news of the Kincaid bequest was announced. Using volunteers to augment its office staff, it had identified what it believed to be every adult resident of the town and was ready to start cutting checks.

Architects had been contacted to bid on the design of the gym and multi-purpose room as well as the park improvements.

With the bulk of the Kincaid funds now in hand, Insley was ready to close the deal with Al Donaldson at Allied. He wanted to do it in person, not on the phone.

Joining Donaldson for the meeting was John Pendergast, Allied's legal counsel. Insley was prepared for a lengthy negotiating session. To his surprise, it was quick and uncomplicated. Allied agreed to the one and a half million sale price subject to one condition: the town forgive nearly six month's of delinquent property taxes. Insley signed before anyone's mind changed.

After all the paperwork was done, Donaldson said: "I know everyone in Waterford hates me and I understand why. But, for what it's worth, I'm glad your town is the beneficiary of the estate and I wish you success in getting someone in the plant who will hire a bunch of your people."

"You're right, Al, you won't be honored with a parade if you show up in Waterford. But I appreciate the way in which you and I have been able to do business."

Insley left Cleveland thinking maybe his town had relied too much on the Kincaid family business. That had to end at some point. Maybe this fresh start, however difficult, would produce a better future. It was up to him to help make that happen.

Soon after the mayor had left his office, Al Donaldson placed a phone call to a Waterford number.

"Is this Jake Walter?"

"Yes, this is Jake. Who's calling?"

"This is Al Donaldson at Allied Manufacturing in Cleveland."

Jake's first thought was that this was a prank call from one of his pals, but he'd stay on the line.

"Jake, we're having quite a few problems trying to get the Kincaid equipment and machinery up and running."

Jake's first unspoken thought: serves you right. You should never have moved our stuff. You should have kept the whole operation here.

"I have a proposal for you to consider. Do you already have another job?"

"No, I've got a couple possibilities, but nothing pinned down."

"Okay, here's my proposal. I know you like living back there, so I'm not suggesting you move your family. I'm prepared to offer you the job of acting general manager of our valve operations. Your contract would run for two years — longer if you and I decide it should. During that time, part of your responsibility will be to identify and groom your successor.

"You were making one hundred and fifty thousand a year at Kincaid. I'm prepared to raise that to one hundred and eighty thousand, plus a housing allowance here and travel expense reimbursement so you can go home to your family most weekends. Also, you'll be immediately eligible to participate in our 401-K plan, and you and your family would be included in our medical insurance package."

Jake didn't interrupt. This was no prank call.

"Talk this over with your family and call me in a couple of days."

After several seconds of silence, Donaldson said, "Jake, we should have offered you a position when we bought the company. We thought we'd be able to get everything up and running without any help. But we haven't; we're in a bit of a bind."

Jake finally spoke up. "Mr. Donaldson ..."

"It's Al, Jake."

" ... Al, I appreciate your call. What if I find I need the help of a few experienced guys from here?"

"How many are you talking about?"

"I won't know until I get there and see what you need. Maybe three or four."

"If you feel they are absolutely necessary and can help train my people, I'm okay with that."

"Thanks, again, for the call. I will talk with my family and get back to you."

"Great. I hope everything works out. Talk with you soon."

Jake's wife, Vivian, came in the den just as the call ended.

"Who was that? Did you get a callback from someone?"

He tried hard but unsuccessfully to keep from smiling.

"No. You'll never guess."

Then he proceeded to take her through chapter and verse of the call.

"Oh, Jake," she said, wrapping her arms around him. "Our prayers have been answered."

Jake waited a day before calling Donaldson; he didn't want to sound desperate.

"I'm delighted," Donaldson said. "When can you start?"

"How soon do you want me?"

"The sooner the better. Today's Thursday. How about Monday?"

"I'll be there."

CHAPTER 61

After sleeping on the good news, Jake decided to phone Florence Treadwell.

"Well, you sound happy," Miss Florence said upon answering the call.

"What would you think if I went to work for Allied?"

"The word that comes to mind is 'traitor'." Florence was famous for her quick wit.

Jake laughed. "I got an offer — out of the blue. Al Donaldson, the president, called me and I agreed to a two-year contract as acting plant manager."

"Oh, Jake, that's wonderful. Tell me more."

He took her through everything — the raise, the housing allowance, travel expense reimbursement, medical coverage ... well, almost everything.

"And," he'd saved this for last, "I may be able to bring several guys with me if I see they're needed. I won't know that until after I'm there and get a grip on what's going on.

"I'm not going to tell a bunch of people here right away, but I wanted you to know. I know you were kidding, but I wouldn't be surprised if some of the guys from the plant will think I'm a traitor. They'll think this was something I knew about when we shut down."

"Oh no, Jake. People know you. They know how straight-up you are. They know you've been looking for a job. They'll be happy for you."

"Vivian and I thought of driving to Charleston to celebrate but we decided instead to have dinner at Darlene's. Can you join us?"

"I'd love to. I happen to have a nice bottle of champagne that's just dying to be opened."

"See you tonight."

It being Saturday morning, Ella Mae, Wally, and Phil headed to Darlene's.

Wally was the first to arrive. Greeted, as always, with Dagwood's "Hi, darlin'" he paused to chat with a couple of friends at the counter before heading for the corner booth.

Darlene followed close behind with a coffee carafe.

"Good morning, Hon. Where are the other two criminals?"

"I expect they're on their way."

"What's new?" It was a question she posed to most everyone.

"Not much. I did apply for one of the cleanup jobs at the plant. I think it'll pay a bit more than the state minimum wage. It'll be tough going in there and seeing all the mess. They just tore stuff out and left all the debris."

"Yeah," Darlene said, "but you'll feel good cleaning it up ... making it all pretty so someone can't resist putting a business in there."

Darlene was always the same. Always positive. The glass was always half full. She didn't tolerate a negative thought for longer than a second. That attitude coupled with her gregarious manner and consistently good food priced reasonably was why people kept coming to Darlene's Dream Diner.

Exchanging greetings with Dagwood, Ella Mae and Phil arrived together.

"What have you two been plotting?" Ella Mae said to Darlene and Wally.

"Wally's gonna buy me out. We're talking about renaming the place Wally's Wonderful World of Pancakes."

"Jeez, Wally," Ella Mae said with a straight face, "do you even know how to make pancakes?"

Wally smiled as he scooted over to make room for his two pals.

"Philly Boy," Darlene said, "you really need to get some new friends. These two are a bad influence." She turned and headed off to the kitchen, not waiting for a spoken response or Ella Mae's "wave."

"So you signed up for the plant cleanup," Ella Mae said to Wally.

"Yep. How about you two."

"I'm going to," Phil responded.

"Well, hell, I may as well, too," Ella Mae said. "My own house is such a mess I should feel right at home."

With all the excitement of the town's newfound wealth, the purchase of the plant, the planned construction at the middle school and park, and the upcoming downtown improvements, they hadn't talked much lately about the unsolved murder.

"I still think Allied got someone to do it," Ella Mae said. "They recognized what a dud he was, what a pompous pain-in-the-ass and decided to save a few bucks and get rid of him. I read somewhere there are still some mobsters in Cleveland who will do those kinds of things. All you got to do is come up with a little money and, 'poof', the guy disappears."

"Why didn't we think of that before Russell sold?" Wally said.

"You're convinced Jake didn't do it?" Phil asked.

"Yeah. He was as pissed as anyone," Ella Mae replied, "and he's a damn good shot, but he'd never do that."

Wally nodded agreement. "I just wonder if our favorite person in the world, Miss Florence, might have hired someone to do the deed. She loved that family, loved the business and couldn't stand what that little twerp had done."

Warming to the subject, Wally continued. "We all know how smart she is. If anyone could pull something like this off, who better than Miss Florence."

Ella Mae hadn't interrupted. Wally had a point. "It just proves what I always say."

"Oh, God, Philly Boy, here it comes," Wally said.

"If you want a job done right, get a woman to do it."

Phil rolled his eyes.

"Stop that," she said, "you know it makes me dizzy."

"We don't agree on all that much," Wally said, "but I'm sure we agree on one thing: this is one crime that needs to go unsolved."

"What crime?" Ella Mae asked. "Since when is it against the law to shoot a skunk? And don't you dare roll your damn eyes, Philly Boy."

He was tempted but restrained himself.

"What's the special occasion?" Darlene asked Florence as she entered the diner carrying the bottle of champagne. "It's not my birthday till November."

"I'm not telling," Florence said. "But I'm having dinner with Jake and Vivian."

"What, are they finally getting married?"

"Oh, Darlene, you always know just the right thing to say."

They hugged before Florence sat down. Florence usually ate at home but she always looked forward to seeing Darlene and enjoyed their back-and-forth exchanges.

Dagwood's "Hi, darlin'" never got old so far as Jake and Vivian were concerned. Vivian would always engage in a more extensive conversation with Dagwood before joining Jake at the table.

"I didn't say anything to Darlene about your job," Florence said in a low voice.

"I'll tell her when the crowd thins out a bit," Jake said. "I'm going to fly up to Cleveland tomorrow afternoon, rent a car, and be on the job first thing Monday."

"You do know if you tell Darlene it will be the talk of the town tomorrow."

"Yeah. But word would spread anyway."

"My wine not good enough for you?" Darlene asked, carrying the champagne and three glasses to the table.

"Bring a fourth glass and have a seat," Jake replied.

"Oh, boy, this is exciting. I'll be right back."

The crowd having thinned, with empty booths on each side, Jake told Darlene the whole story.

"Well, I'll be damn," she said. "Maybe they're not as dumb as I thought they were up in Cleveland. You'll set them straight. But if they're not nice to you, I bet you know how to sabotage the finishing mill."

That provoked a laugh from Jake, Vivian and Florence. Leave it to Darlene to lighten any conversation.

"Is it okay if I tell some folks?" Darlene asked.

"Sure, but don't mention the part about the possibility I might be able to get a few folks from here to join me. I don't want to get any hopes up because I don't know what I'm going to find when I get up there."

"I'm happy for you, Jake," Darlene said. "Vivian, with him out of your hair during the week, you can come see me more often."

"I'll do it ... to see you and talk with Dagwood."

CHAPTER 62

Two weeks later, the cleanup work at the plant was well under way. Forty former employees were at work eight hours a day, forty hours a week, and being paid a couple of bucks above the state minimum wage. The toughest part was breaking up what seemed like hundreds of large chunks of concrete created when casting and rolling equipment had been removed from the floor. Once removed, most of the chunks were hauled down to a relatively remote part of the Maplethorn and used to reinforce its erosion-damaged river bank.

After that, new steel reinforced flooring had to be poured in the damaged areas. Meantime, all the plant offices were being repainted and floors retiled. A smaller team of eight was at work restoring the lawn and freshening up the plantings around most of the perimeter of the building.

The hope remained that one company would come in and take the entire space, so they didn't make any structural changes.

Yet to be done was a complete power washing of the building's exterior to enhance its eye appeal. That part didn't need much help. Junior Kincaid and his father had been sticklers about the plant's appearance. Most people in Waterford took pride in the appearance of their homes and yards, and the Kincaids made sure the plant reflected that same look.

Work at the park was under way, flower boxes had been installed along Cedar Street, and groundbreaking for the new gym and multi-purpose room was two weeks away.

Mayor Insley and the Town Council decided to combine the park dedication and ground breaking with the unveiling of the refurbished plant. The Governor, both U.S. Senators, and Congressman Bosworth had been invited, along with folks from Economic Development.

The plan was to have a parade or motorcade of sorts, starting up near the Interstate, with a stop at the park, then up the beautified Cedar Street to the middle school site for the groundbreaking and speeches, and finally to the like-new-appearing plant, where Darlene would cater a buffet lunch.

While all of this was going on, most of the folks who previously had good jobs at the plant remained unemployed, so Waterford had contracted with the Parkersburg Food Bank to set up a field operation in an unoccupied warehouse just north of town.

Unemployment checks were still being received, and all but a few folks were tightening their belts and staying put in Waterford.

Insley and the Council had discussed the possibility of another cash payment to residents but hoped they could avoid it. During the first round, a number of individuals who lived in Waterford but worked elsewhere or were unaffected by the plant closure had generously contributed all or a part of their payment back to the city.

Where else but in Waterford would that happen? Insley thought to himself. Within ten days after the checks had been sent out, donations totaling more than two hundred thousand had been received. He made a note to remind himself to mention in his groundbreaking remarks these donations and the foundation the town had established to accept them.

Several days after arriving at Allied, it became clear to Jake that he needed three or four experienced hands from Waterford to get Allied on the right path. Donaldson approved the additions. They, like Jake, would be hired for a specific length of time. In their case, for six months, with an option to extend if necessary.

Jake knew who he wanted. A former foreman from finishing, one from maintenance, another from engineering, and Wally from casting. All would be charged with getting the operation running smoothly as well as training their successors.

Wally broke the news to Ella Mae and Phil at breakfast.

"I'm not having lunch with you two on Tuesday or Thursday for awhile. I'll try to make Saturdays."

"Was it something I said that offended your tender ears?" Ella Mae asked.

"What's up?" Phil added before Wally could answer Ella Mae.

"I'm going up to Cleveland to help Jake for six months."

"Jeez," Ella Mae said, showing her best semi-sour, wide-eyed expression, "he must really be desperate."

"Thanks for the vote of confidence, pretty lady."

"Man, that's great," Phil said.

Wally then described what he and the other three from Kincaid would be doing. "I expect we'll be able to come home most weekends.

"Phil and I will decide whether we want to see your sorry ass on Saturdays," Ella Mae said.

"Let me know what you decide," Wally said with a smile. He was looking forward to getting back to work in a job he knew well and working for a guy he liked and respected. But he'd miss Ella Mae's abuse, Phil's good company, Darlene's cooking, and Dagwood's hellos and goodbyes.

Tuesday and Thursday breakfast without Wally seemed strange.

Phil said it was probably his imagination but Dagwood seemed to be looking past him for Wally. Even Ella Mae's manner was somewhat subdued.

Sitting in their booth and just sort of looking at each other she saw Frank Wharton come in.

"Chief," she hollered. "Get over here and talk with us. We've lost our cell mate."

Frank had intended to pick up some doughnuts and take them back to the office. Then he thought, what the heck, I can sit down for a few minutes.

"What's new on the crime-fighting front?" Ella Mae asked, perking up a bit.

"Not a lot now that you've stopped drinking." Frank knew how to give as well as take from Ella Mae.

"Is it against the law to give a cop the bird?"

"It depends on the cop. Phil, I know how Ella Mae is. How are you doing?"

"Not too bad. With the unemployment comp, the money from the city, and an assortment of odd jobs, we're doing okay, keeping a roof over our heads."

"So, your compatriot is up in Cleveland helping Jake."

"Yep. He called the other night. Said he was getting a handle on things. But he also said he was surprised how little those guys know about the valve business."

"Maybe they'll end up hiring more of you. Selfishly, I hope they don't. We kind of like having you around. You think they'd ever hire Ella Mae?"

Phil laughed and, yes, rolled his eyes.

"They wouldn't dare hire me," she said. "I'd lure that president guy, what's his name, Donaldson, over to one of the casting pits and push him in."

"I don't doubt it for a minute," Frank responded.

"Hey, Chief," Ella Mae said, "Darlene gives us a ten-cent discount if there's three of us. Why don't you join us on Tuesday and Thursday? You in place of Wally wouldn't be too much of a downgrade. Plus, all those sugary doughnuts are playing hell with your Adonis body."

"Thank you for such a kind invitation and compliment. Maybe I'll see you here on Thursday. That is unless you're already in one of my overnight holding cells."

Frank didn't wait for Ella Mae to respond. He got up, flicked Phil's hat down over his eyes and headed off to the front door to pick up his doughnuts and bid farewell to Dagwood.

Phil just shook his head and laughed, trying hard not to roll his eyes.

CHAPTER 63

The day Waterford had chosen for the groundbreaking and other events was a crystal-clear summer day. The Governor had sent his regrets, but U.S. Senator Winston Moorland was coming as was Congressman Bosworth. Moorland was a Republican and Bosworth a Democrat. They didn't especially like each other but would behave at such a happy event because both were up for reelection.

Mayor Insley would deliver welcoming remarks but he had recruited Michael Obitz to preside over the day's events. As a former Attorney General and the founder of the largest law firm in the state, not to mention being a major financial contributor to both Moorland and Bosworth, Obitz was a popular choice.

Much of the work at the park was completed and Senator Moorland dutifully unveiled the new sign naming it for the Kincaids.

Cedar Street was abloom as never before, and parents and children waved American and West Virginia flags as the motorcade crept by.

The lot for the new gym and multi-purpose room had been neatly cleared and enough shiny shovels for the groundbreaking photo op had been provided for each Council member, Obitz, Moorland, Bosworth, the ED department head, and Mayor Insley.

Michael Obitz's speech outshined those of the Senator, Congressman, and ED representative, reminding more than a few in the audience that he would have made a great Governor or Senator.

Seated, unobtrusively, in the third row with Attorneys Sherman Wilson and A. J. Washington was Julia Jamison and Russell's and her son, Richard, now four. At her request, they wouldn't be introduced. But they had been at the park for the naming ceremony and Julia had made sure her son appreciated the significance of the event.

The lawn and plant-lined driveway leading to the main entrance of the plant looked like something out of a Southern Living magazine, and the offices and plant floor inside were immaculate.

The words "Waterford Proud" streamed above the head table.

Darlene outdid herself. She and her team had gone to the diner at three that morning to start preparing the food. The buffet featured her special-recipe fried chicken, house-made potato and macaroni salads, deep-fried okra, and carrots and peas. Pitchers of sweet tea and tubs of Dr Pepper and Squirt were strategically placed at various locations in the plant. Huge sheet cakes reiterating the "Waterford Proud" message completed the feast.

Mayor Insley sought out Julia Jamison and young Richard, introduced them to Senator Moorland and Congressman Bosworth, and showed them the office where the boy's great-grandfather, grandfather, and father had worked. Michael Obitz joined them and told a smiling Richard he had "a great mom."

It had been a day to remember. Insley and all others who had worked to make it a success were exhausted but proud they had pulled it off.

CHAPTER 64

Three weeks had passed since the groundbreaking, and the slabs had been poured for the new gym complex. Work at the park was finished and families were making great use of it, even as the weather turned hot and humid.

Steve Insley was in his hardware store when he got the call. Economic Development had been contacted by Hamilton Manufacturing Corporation, a major producer of office and commercial furniture, based in Boise, Idaho. They were interested in locating a factory closer to the Midwest and Eastern markets, and they wanted to take a look at the Kincaid plant.

"Fantastic," Insley said. "You tell me when they want to come and we'll meet them at the airport."

"How's day after tomorrow?"

"Couldn't be better," Insley replied. "Let me know the details. Meantime, I'll get busy making things ready."

Insley hung up the apron he always wore when working at the store, told his two employees they were in charge, and sprinted across the street to the town hall.

The other four members of the Town Council were available, so they set about drawing up plans for the visit. They'd show off the park, the downtown area, and the progress being made on the gym/multi-purpose complex. Assuming the visitors had the time, they'd have

Darlene cater something, either at the plant or in the Council conference room.

Insley had consulted with an industrial realtor friend already and determined a range of leases based on length and comparables in the state.

Two representatives from Hamilton Manufacturing were due to arrive at Charleston's airport at one fifteen. Insley would meet them, take them on the mini-tour, and proceed to the plant, where several members of the Town Council would join them.

Company vice presidents, Jonathan Foster and Peter McGowan, stepped into the terminal and were greeted by Insley.

Insley did most of the talking on the drive up the Interstate to Waterford. He drove slowly by the park, up Cedar Street, which looked as inviting as it had several weeks before, and to the gym site where about 20 laborers were at work. His visitors, gazing out at one mountain ridge after another, hadn't said much.

As they drove up the drive to the plant's entrance, he could sense their interest growing.

Introductions at the plant were accomplished quickly and the tour began. Insley sensed they liked the layout, the openness, the fact that the offices were modest but attractive.

But still, not many questions or feedback. He began wondering if he was doing as much as he could to stimulate their interest.

Having waited as long as he could, he decided to ask the question.

"Well, gentlemen, what do you think?"

Foster deferred to McGowan. "You have a nice facility here. We've been looking for rail and highway access, and you have both. What about workers?"

Insley was encouraged. "We've got a bunch of people I'd put up against any other group. They'd need some training, but they are smart, adaptable, and reliable. When Kincaid had the plant, turnover was next-to-nothing."

"Training is not a problem," Foster said, "we'd do that. We do that wherever we locate."

"More than 200 people worked here at the time Allied shut it down," Insley said. "Most all of them are still here, anxious to go back to work."

McGowan looked at Foster, who nodded.

"We're looking to lease a property, not buy it." "We'd prefer to lease," Insley said. "We are new owners of the plant and are happy we were able to acquire it."

A number of other questions were asked and answered. The only commitment made was that McGowan would contact Insley a few days after he got back to Idaho.

Insley offered the option of dinner in the Council offices or in Charleston where McGowan and Foster had overnight accommodations.

"The Economic Development people told us about a restaurant near here that serves the world's best fried chicken and peach pie," McGowan said.

"I happen to know the place," Insley replied, a smile beaming across his face. "Let me make a quick phone call."

Darlene had reserved the large booth in the corner furthest from the front door. It would easily accommodate Insley and his friends, and she would leave another booth and a couple of nearby tables open so they could talk in semi-privacy.

Initially taken aback by Dagwood's loud "Hi, darlin', they lingered for a moment by his cage as he blurted out "Big news!"

Insley introduced Darlene to his visitors. "Fellas," she began, "welcome to the best damn restaurant in West Virginia. What can I get you?"

After they said they wanted the fried chicken, she kidded, "I'm sorry, we're all out of chicken; how about calves liver?"

Insley could see Darlene and Dagwood were having the desired effect. His visitors were having a great time.

On the drive back to Charleston, Foster said, "That woman's incredible. I thought we had some good food in Boise, and we do. But that chicken and that peach pie. Absolutely unbelievable."

They reviewed briefly a few details they'd discussed at the plant and, later, at dinner. Insley offered to meet them for breakfast but they declined, saying they had an early flight. He didn't ask if they were headed back to Idaho or were going to check out other possible locations.

Driving back to Waterford, Insley felt good. The discussions at the plant had gone well. He believed Waterford had everything they wanted. But if McGowan or Foster had any doubts, Darlene had provided the clincher.

Insley phoned Economic Development the next morning to brief them on how the visit had gone. They agreed it sounded promising.

However, a week passed without a callback. Insley had expected to hear something sooner. Anything. A yes, no, or we are thinking about it.

Then the call came, directly to Insley, at his store. It was Peter McGowan.

"Steve, we need to talk. Jonathan (Foster) and I are tired of looking at locations. We've covered a lot of ground. We want to come to Waterford."

For a second or two, Insley wasn't sure whether McGowan meant he wanted to visit again or he was committing, on the spot, to locate in Waterford. He hesitated long enough for McGowan to continue.

"We'll have our legal department begin drafting a proposed agreement. Who should we work with at your end?"

My God, he thought. They're coming. We're going to be making office furniture right here in Waterford, West Virginia.

Michael Obitz had committed to Insley that his office, pro bono, would handle any legal matters relating to leasing the plant, so Insley provided Obitz's number. He told McGowan a little about Obitz's background and accomplishments. Insley's hand was shaking as he scribbled a note reminding him to alert Obitz to expect a call.

"This is great news, Peter. We won't make any announcement or confirm any discussions until you say it's okay."

"Good. We've got some work to do before finalizing everything."

McGowan had mentioned during the initial visit they expected to hire one hundred and fifty people at first and grow within the next eight or nine months to as many as three hundred. Insley wanted to pin that down.

"That's our plan. Once all the papers are signed and the deal is done, we'll come back to you with the timing for our interviewing. The skills levels we find in the people we interview will help determine how long the training takes. Meantime, we can be equipping the plant."

"I'll tell Michael Obitz to expect your call, and the Council and I will look forward to working with you and Jonathan and whomever else to make this happen. Waterford won't disappoint you. That, I can guarantee."

"Great, Steve. Talk with you soon."

Normally soft spoken, the mayor let loose with a holler immediately after hanging up, followed by a little dance. At first his two employees at the store thought he might have dropped something heavy on his foot. That happened sometimes in a hardware store. Then they saw his smile and knew it must have something to do with to their beloved town.

+++

Insley soon learned that Hamilton Manufacturing moved quickly once they had reached a decision. Within a couple of weeks, a fifteen-year lease had been agreed to.

"Unbelievable" was the word heard most around town. The cycle that had started less than a year before with shock, fear, and depression had turned into hope, optimism and self-confidence.

The media couldn't get enough of the story — it was a rare dose of good news in a part of the country that seemed to get more than its share of the other kind.

With the lease finalized, Hamilton began moving equipment into the plant so it would be ready for the training sessions and, later, for production of furniture.

Two weeks later came the notice that Hamilton was taking applications and granting interviews. That first day, the line stretched all the way down the long driveway to Cedar Street as more than four hundred applied. The second day, the number was nearly two hundred, and the third and final day, another one hundred. They came from several counties around and from Ohio as well.

Unspoken was Hamilton's intention to hire mostly ex-Kincaid employees so long as they met its criteria. In discussing this with Insley and others, McGowan and Foster had been impressed with what they heard about Kincaid's ex-workforce. Also, hiring locally would help build good relations with the hometown.

A little over one hundred had been hired the first two weeks, and almost immediately began paid training. Another fifty followed soon thereafter. Of the total, one hundred and thirty-five were ex-Kincaid employees.

Phil was among those hired in the first batch, followed by Ella Mae in the second.

Waterford clearly had got its mojo back.

Although Darlene's breakfast business dropped off a bit because folks were now working, dinner business was booming as job-seekers invaded Waterford and locals celebrated their future.

No more Tuesday and Thursday breakfasts for the now-employed Wally and Ella Mae, but Saturday was mandatory.

Whether real or imagined, Darlene was convinced Dagwood was happier. She thought it was probably because all the new folks coming in doted over him.

Frank Wharton joined Ella Mae, Phil, and, sometimes, Wally for breakfast on those Saturdays he wasn't out hunting or fishing.

Ella Mae tried unsuccessfully to hide how happy she was. "Who says you can't teach an old dog new tricks," Ella Mae blurted out. "Six months ago I was pouring molten metal; now I'm learning to make classy office furniture. I never thought I'd be back in school — not at my age."

Having impressed both the interviewer and training staff, Phil was hired on as a foreman, making a couple of thousand dollars a year more than he had made at Kincaid.

"Damn," he said to Ella Mae, "I was beginning to think the rest of my life would be spent mowing lawns and unplugging toilets."

Darlene was flying high because Mayor Insley had said her chicken and peach pie sealed the deal with Hamilton

Manufacturing. Flattered at first, she began to believe it was true after "that handsome, young Mr. McGowan" kept ordering both of the items whenever he came to town.

CHAPTER 65

Now with a trained work force of one hundred and fifty and plans to recruit and train another like amount, and with the quality of furniture being produced meeting Hamilton's high-quality standard, the time had come for a celebration.

It would be an Open House, where families and townspeople could tour the plant, dine on hot dogs and hamburgers cooked by Darlene and her staff, and listen to some good old country music.

A crackling thunderstorm the night before yielded a cooler, cloudless day. The plant tours were over by five, dinner started at six, and the music extended into the night.

Insley and Peter McGowan had become fast friends. McGowan, his wife and two children had moved from Idaho to Waterford, living temporarily in a rented house but planning to build on the outskirts of town.

For Waterford, the roller coaster ride was over and a return to the pleasures of living in a small but thriving West Virginia town was assured.

All but forgotten was the reality that Russell Kincaid had been shot and found floating in the Maplethorn River less than a year ago.

But it would never be forgotten by three people.

The hour was getting late and the country band was wrapping up what would be their final song, "Country

Roads," the John Denver hit that West Virginia adopted as its anthem.

The three had seen each other several times during the evening but always in the presence of others. Now, Miss Florence and Ella Mae were off in a darkened corner. Frank walked over, looking over his shoulder to be sure no one was following. Then he gave each a hug.

"Do you suppose we'll go to Hell for what we did?" Florence asked, her voice barely above a whisper.

"If we do," Ella Mae said, "we'll have some explaining to do to Russell because he's already there."

Frank restrained himself from laughing. "Living a lie isn't easy, is it?"

"Like anything else, it takes practice," Ella Mae answered.

"I'm sure glad Junior told me about that letter and its contents before he went fishing in Alaska. If he hadn't, I wouldn't have known his wishes and we wouldn't have had to do what we did," Florence said. "Do you two still believe it was justified?"

"I sure as hell do," Ella Mae replied.

"Yes," Frank said, "but a court wouldn't."

"Do you think someone will ever figure this out?" Florence asked.

"If they do, it would make a pretty good book, maybe even a movie," Ella Mae said, striking a pose.

Florence shook her head and looked at Frank. "I can do without the fame. How about you, Frank?"

"For sure. Take care, ladies."

ABOUT THE AUTHOR

Bob Irelan's commitment to writing began in earnest when, as a college student, he majored in journalism, and it grew steadily throughout his career.

Following 10 years of newspaper and magazine reporting and editing, including stints at The Wall Street Journal and Nation's Business magazine in Washington, DC, he spent 32 years in public relations for a Fortune 500 family of companies. As a corporate officer, he directed the companies' internal and external communications for the last 12 of those years.

In retirement, he taught a public relations course for two years at University of the Pacific and for five years at University of California, Davis, Extension. The Sacramento Public Relations Association honored him with its "Lifetime Achievement Award" in 2005.

***Justifiable* is his second novel.** His first, *Angel's Truth - One Teenager's Quest for Justice,* placed second in fiction at the Northern California Publishers and Authors' 25th Annual Awards in 2019.

Bob has lived in Maryland, California (three different times), West Virginia, and Texas, He currently lives in Rancho Murieta, California.

Shortly after completing this novel, Jocko, the handsome cat pictured on the back cover, passed away at the age of 18. Ever present as the author typed away, Jocko's contribution was a calming influence and a companionship beyond description.

ALSO BY BOB IRELAN

Angel Gonzales is charged with heinous crimes that law enforcement, the media, and most folks in Richmond, Texas, and surrounding communities are certain he committed.

The crimes and trial dwarf anything that has happened in that part of the Lone Star state in anyone's memory.

When, against all odds, the jury renders "not guilty" verdicts, shock escalates to anger. In the minds of many, justice has failed, and a brutal criminal is being set free.

For Angel and his court-appointed public defender, Marty Booker, being judged "not guilty" isn't enough.

Together and with help from an unanticipated source, they attempt to prove Angel's innocence. In the process, they butt up against prejudice, deceit, and a sheriff and district attorney who put politics, ambition, expedience, and arrogance above responsibility to do their jobs.

It's a story of horror, hatred, belief, and persistence - a story of a Mexican-American teenager who nearly loses his life on the way to becoming a man.

Available on Amazon Kindle and in print and in fine bookstores everywhere.